D0829590

Abby forgot to breathe.

Her entire body went liquid with pleasure. When she cried out, he ripped at her sweater, dragging it and her bra over her head in short order, tangling her hair and leaving her naked from the waist up.

Abby knew they were careening down a dangerous slope. "Duncan, please."

He froze, his chest heaving. He reared up on one elbow. His free hand was at her waistband, struggling with the fastening on her pants.

His eyes were open. In the faint illumination from the bathroom light, they glittered with intent. "Are ye asking me to stop, lass?"

It was up to her. She could stand up and walk away, and nothing would happen. The hushed silence after his question seemed to last forever, though probably only seconds passed.

She was defeated by his raw need and her own yearning. Everything inside her wanted to give him peace and release. She wanted that and more for herself.

She wasn't going to have Duncan Stewart for any kind of happily-ever-after. But she could have tonight.

She *would* have it.

"No." She swallowed hard, trying to find her breath, her courage. "Don't stop."

* * *

On Temporary Terms is part of the Highland Heroes duet from *USA TODAY* bestselling author Janice Maynard!

Dear Reader,

I was lucky growing up. My childhood wasn't perfect, but it was pretty darn good. I lost my dad too soon (he was forty-two), but I had my mom, and I had her mother, my grandmother. That relationship with my grandmother was one I treasure even now, many years after her death.

My hero, Duncan Stewart, adores his grandmother and is willing to do almost anything for her, but he feels guilty for not being able to be 100 percent on board with the whole self-sacrifice thing. When he meets Abby, he has no idea that she is dealing with some pretty difficult situations of her own.

Sometimes love comes like a summer rain, gentle and beautiful. But sometimes love is borne out of hardship and shared emotion. Duncan and Abby are thrown together in the midst of a whirlwind that neither of them expects.

This book is very special to me because the themes come from deep in the heart of our shared human emotion. I hope it speaks to you as it did to me.

If you have a moment, please connect with me on Facebook and/or Goodreads and let me know what you think about Duncan and Abby's story.

Thanks so much for your interest in my books. I treasure each one of you!

Fondly,

Janice Maynard

JANICE MAYNARD

——

ON TEMPORARY TERMS

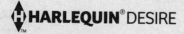

Recycling programs
for this product may
not exist in your area.

ISBN-13: 978-1-335-97164-7

On Temporary Terms

Printed in U.S.A.

www.Harlequin.com

USA TODAY bestselling author **Janice Maynard** loved books and writing even as a child. But it took multiple rejections before she sold her first manuscript. Since 2002, she has written over forty-five books and novellas. Janice lives in east Tennessee with her husband, Charles. They love hiking, traveling and spending time with family.

You can connect with Janice at janicemaynard.com, Twitter.com/janicemaynard, Facebook.com/janicemaynardreaderpage, Facebook.com/janicesmaynard and Instagram.com/janicemaynard.

Books by Janice Maynard

Harlequin Desire

The Kavanaghs of Silver Glen

A Not-So-Innocent Seduction
Baby for Keeps
Christmas in the Billionaire's Bed
Twins on the Way
Second Chance with the Billionaire
How to Sleep with the Boss
For Baby's Sake

Highland Heroes

His Heir, Her Secret
On Temporary Terms

Visit her Author Profile page at Harlequin.com, or janicemaynard.com, for more titles.

For everyone whose childhood
was not storybook perfect.
For everyone whose parents were
embarrassing or hurtful or not present at all.
May you find love and acceptance in other
relationships and know that you are not
defined by the difficulties and struggles
of the past. God bless...

One

Abby Hartmann liked her job most days. Being a small-town lawyer included more good weeks than bad. But on this particular Saturday morning—the dreaded once-a-month half day—things were definitely looking up. With her palms damp and her heartbeat fluttering, she smoothed her skirt and waved a hand toward the wingbacked chair opposite her large cherry desk. "Have a seat, Mr. Stewart."

She straightened a few papers and folders, and took a deep breath. The man whose sheer presence shrank the square footage of her office was a commanding figure. Close-cropped dark brown hair. Deep chocolate eyes. A lean, athletic body. And a stillness about him. An intensity. As if at any moment he could leap across the small space separating them, grab her up and kiss her witless. He seemed almost dangerous, which made no sense at all. Maybe it was the quivering physical awareness making her restless.

Her reaction was disconcerting. Just because the guy had a sexy Scottish accent and a seriously hot body was no reason to lose her composure. Besides, no matter how attractive, the Scotsman embodied the rich, entitled male arrogance that set her teeth on edge. She'd met dozens like him, albeit not Scottish. Men who took what they wanted and didn't mind who they left behind in the dust.

Duncan Stewart seemed uncomfortable as well, but perhaps for a different reason. "I'm not sure why I'm here," he said. "My grandmother likes to be mysterious at times."

Abby managed a smile, though she was entirely off her game. "Isobel Stewart is an original, that's for sure. It's no big secret. She's updated her will and wanted me to go over it with you. Do you mind my asking why you've decided to relocate from Scotland to North Carolina?"

He raised an eyebrow. "I'd have thought that was obvious. Granny is well past ninety. Grandda has been gone almost a year now. You know my brother, Brody, has a new wife and baby, and they've moved back to Skye."

"I had heard that. Your sister-in-law owned the bookstore down the street, Dog-Eared Pages—right?"

"Aye. Since none of us have been successful in persuading Granny to sell out and leave Candlewick, *somebody* has to be here to look after her."

"That's astonishingly generous on your part, Mr. Stewart. Not many men I know, young or old, would put their lives on hold for their grandmothers."

* * *

Duncan couldn't decide if the odd note in the lawyer's voice was admiration or sarcasm. "I didn't really have a choice," he said. His reluctance to play a part in this drama shamed him. Still, he was going to do the right thing. It didn't mean he was comfortable with the lawyer's praise. The woman sitting across the desk from him seemed harmless, but he would be in no rush to trust her. He didn't have a very high opinion of solicitors in general, or of the entire legal profession for that matter. He'd seen too much nastiness during his parents' divorce.

Abby Hartmann stared at him. "*Everyone* has choices, Mr. Stewart. In some instances, I might think you were in it for the money, but your grandmother has told me more than I ever needed to know about you and your brother. I'm aware that you're extremely comfortable financially with or without your share in Stewart Properties."

Duncan winced. "I'm guessing she also told you our father isn't getting a dime, and she made it sound like a big deal."

Abby gave him a small smile and nodded. "She might have mentioned it in passing. I Googled him. Your dad has a dozen thriving art galleries all over Great Britain, right? I doubt he cares about his mother's money."

"He and Granny have a complicated relationship. It works best when they both live on different continents."

The lawyer grimaced, her face shadowed for a moment. "I can certainly understand that."

Though Duncan had not wanted to come here

today, he found himself willing to prolong the conversation for no other reason than to enjoy the lawyer's company. He'd been expecting a middle-aged woman in a gray suit and glasses with precise opinions and tightly controlled behaviors. What he'd found instead was a barely five-foot-three curvy bombshell.

Maybe he had formed too many opinions of female solicitors from television and movies, but Abby Hartmann broke the mold. According to the diplomas on the wall behind her head, she appeared to be in her late twenties. She was warm and appealing, and nothing about her was rigid. Her hair was chin length and wildly curly, neither red nor blond, but an appealing amalgam of both.

She wore a black knee-length pencil skirt that showcased a rounded ass and beautiful legs that were now hidden beneath her desk. The buttons on her red shirt struggled to contain her stellar breasts. In fact, Duncan had a difficult time keeping his eyes off that tantalizing sight.

He wasn't a Neanderthal. He respected women. Still, holy hell. Abby Hartmann was stacked. Her attire was not provocative. She had left only the first two buttons of her top undone. A tiny gold cross dangled at the upper slopes of her breasts. But that cleavage…

Moving restlessly, he cleared his throat and wished he hadn't declined the bottle of water she had offered him earlier. "I love my grandmother, Ms. Hartmann. She and my grandfather built Stewart Properties from the ground up. In her eyes, it keeps him alive."

"Call me Abby, please. She told me your grandfather chose to change his surname to her maiden name in order to keep the Stewart clan name going. That's pretty extraordinary, don't you think? Particularly for a man of his generation?"

Duncan shrugged. "They had a grand love affair, one of those you read about in books. He adored her and vice versa. From his point of view, she gave up everything for him—her family, her homeland. I suppose it was his way of saying he wanted her to have something in return."

"I think it's lovely."

"But?"

"I didn't say but…"

Duncan grinned. "I'm pretty sure I heard a *but* coming."

Abby flushed. "I don't mean to discount your grandparents' devotion, but I doubt things like that happen anymore. The passionate love affairs. The epic gestures. The decades-long marriages."

"You're awfully young for such pessimism, aren't you?"

"And you don't know me well enough to make that judgment," she snapped.

He blinked. The lawyer had a temper. "My apologies. We should get on with the will. I don't want to take up too much of your time."

Abby groaned audibly. "Sorry. Hot-button issue. Perhaps we could back up a step or two. And yes, we'll go over the will, but first, one more question. If your grandmother left Scotland to settle here with your grandfather, how did you wind up a Scotsman?"

"My grandparents had only one child, my father. Dad was always fascinated with his Scottish roots. As soon as he was an adult, he moved to the Highlands and never looked back. Scotland is the only home Brody and I have ever known, except for the occasional visits here to Candlewick."

"I know about your brother's boating business in Skye. What did you do there?"

"I was his CFO." He stopped and sighed. "Still am, I guess. We don't know how long this hiatus will be. I've urged him to replace me permanently. It's not fair for the business to limp along indefinitely."

"I'm sorry. This must be a very challenging time for you."

The genuine kindness in her soft gray eyes warmed him. For the first time in days, he believed he might survive this sea change in his life. "Not as hard as losing Grandda. That shook all of us. He was an amazing man."

"Yes, he was. I didn't know him well, but his reputation in Candlewick is impressive. People around here would do most anything for your grandmother. She is beloved, you know."

"I do know. That's one reason none of us had the heart to insist she leave. That and the fact that we would have had to pick her up bodily and carry her onto a plane kicking and screaming."

"Boggles the mind, doesn't it?"

"You don't know the half of it. When a cantankerous old Scotswoman sets her mind to something, there's no choice but to get out of her way."

"I don't envy you the task of keeping her in line." Abby smiled, her eyes alight with humor.

Duncan tried not to notice the way her breasts moved when she shifted in her chair. "Would you have dinner with me one evening?" he asked impulsively.

The lawyer stilled. The air in the room hushed. Even Duncan was momentarily abashed. He was not at all an impulsive kind of man.

Abby gnawed her lip. "I'm not sure that would be ethical."

Duncan seized on the weakness in her argument and the fact that she hadn't given him an unequivocal no. "You're not *my* lawyer," he said.

"Perhaps I should have been more clear from the beginning," she replied, looking rattled and mildly alarmed. "My colleague, Mr. Chester, has been your grandparents' lawyer for a very long time. But he's on medical leave at the moment following serious heart surgery. I've been charged with handling your grandmother's affairs in the short term. We have a client who is very interested in purchasing Stewart Properties. It's a cash offer."

Duncan's cynicism kicked in, laced with a big dose of disappointment. Lawyers were snakes, every single one of them. "Not interested."

Abby's gaze narrowed. "It's a very fair offer."

"I don't care. I don't want to hear about it. Granny doesn't want to sell."

"I thought you were looking out for her best interests," the lawyer said, a bite in her voice.

"I definitely am. So it raises a big red flag for me when her lawyers try to force her to sell a company she loves."

"Mr. Chester cares about your grandmother's well-being. We all do."

"How touching."

"Are you being intentionally rude and cynical, or does it come naturally to you? I resent having my professional ethics called into question."

"And I resent people who try to take advantage of an old woman."

"How does making her extremely wealthy take advantage of her?"

"Granny doesn't need more money. She has plenty."

"No one *ever* has enough money, Mr. Stewart. Trust me."

Duncan heard something in that remark…something wounded and weary. But he chose not to pursue it at the moment. Despite his entirely logical antipathy toward lawyers and the inescapable notion that he should stay far away from this woman, he circled back to his original proposal. "Have dinner with me," he said.

"No."

Duncan frowned. "Think of it as community service. I'm lonely. I don't know a single person in town other than my ancient grandmother and you. Have pity on me, Abby Hartmann. And call me Duncan. I feel as if we know each other already."

"Don't lay it on too thick, *Duncan*. I'll think about it. But don't push me. Besides, why would you want to have dinner with a snake-in-the-grass lawyer? I'm getting very mixed signals from you."

Duncan held up his hands. "I'll no' mention it again. At least not for a few days. And you have a fair point. Now how about that will?"

Abby seemed relieved at the change of subject. Duncan entertained himself by watching her shift back into lawyer mode. She clicked a button on her computer, consulted a notepad, and opened a legal-size folder, muttering to herself charmingly as she did so.

He'd always been attracted to smart women. Something about their unwillingness to put up with crap from men challenged his masculinity and brought out his fighting instincts. Abby was no pushover. Though he was well aware that his arousal was not one-sided, he was not foolish enough to assume that meant an easy conquest.

If he wanted the lushly rounded lawyer in his bed, she would make him work for it. He liked that. A lot...

At last, she slid a second folder across the desk to him and opened it. "Here you go. You've seen an earlier version of this. One significant addition is an *escape* clause, if you will. After twenty-four months, if you're unhappy and still want to go home, your grandmother has agreed to sell Stewart Properties and accompany you back to Scotland. I've flagged the changes and the spots where you'll add your name. Your brother and grandmother have already signed."

Duncan frowned. "They have?"

"Yes. Brody needed to do it before he left. Your grandmother came with him."

"Why did no one tell me?" Duncan had a bad feeling in his gut.

"I'm telling you now."

Duncan scanned the paragraphs of legal-speak, searching for the alterations that necessitated this visit. His heart pounded. The tiny pink "flags" denoting spots requiring his signature mocked him. Surely he wasn't reading the document correctly. "I don't understand," he said slowly. "Granny told us she was leaving her company to Brody and me fifty-fifty."

"In light of recent developments—Brody's marriage, your relocation to America—your grandmother and your brother thought it would be only fair to change the split to eighty-twenty. You've given up your career and your life in Scotland. They want to make sure you don't suffer for that decision."

"I made the choice willingly," he insisted. "I didn't ask for anything in return. This is preposterous. I won't sign it."

"Have you *met* your grandmother?" Abby asked jokingly, her expression sympathetic. "I can assure you she won't be moved on this point. Besides, you're not getting a free ride by any means. You'll earn your money. The company is enormous and complex. I'm told that one of the two managers is moving to the West Coast any day now to be closer to family. Your grandmother wants to be involved, but she is no longer physically capable of an intensive workday. The future success or failure of Stewart Properties will rest on your shoulders."

"Thanks for the pep talk."

"We have a saying in this country, Duncan. *The buck stops here.* Your decision to move to Candlewick and look after your grandmother is not going to be easy. Dealing with elderly people never is. But you'll have the added stress of running a multimillion-dollar company, give or take a few zeroes."

"Again, you suck at this."

She grinned. "My job is to clarify the gray areas."

"Consider them clarified." Duncan felt mildly ill. "I have a strong urge to leave it all to Brody."

"I don't think he would take it."

"Great. Just great."

"Think of it as an adventure."

He signed the requisite spots and shoved the folder away. "There. It's done. I hope I can count on you in the weeks and months to come."

Abby's soft pink lips, lightly coated in gloss, opened and shut. "For legal advice?"

Duncan sat back in his chair and smiled at her, letting her see, for the very first time, the extent of his male interest. "For everything."

Abby went through the rest of her workday in a daze. She fluctuated between excitement that Duncan Stewart had asked her out on a date and the absolute certainty that he had been joking.

Fortunately, she had dinner plans with her best friend, Lara Finch. The two of them met at Abby's house and rode together the twenty miles to Claremont. There were places to eat in Candlewick, charming mom-and-pop establishments, plus the usual pizza joints, but for privacy and a change of scenery, it was nice to make the extra effort.

Over chicken crepes, Lara quizzed her. "Something's up, Abby girl. Your face is all red, and you've barely said a word since we got here."

"I talked in the car."

"Correction," Lara said. "*I* talked in the car. You did a lot of listening."

"You're the designated driver. I've had a glass of wine. That's why my neck is hot, and I'm flushed."

"Abby!" Lara gave her a look that said she wasn't going to be put off.

"Oh, fine. If you must know, I met a guy today."

Lara put down her fork, leaned back in her chair and stared. Speechless.

Abby winced. "It's not *that* unusual, is it?"

"The last time you mentioned a man to me was sometime around the turn of the century."

"We didn't even know each other at the turn of the century," Abby pointed out dryly.

Lara picked up her fork again and waved it in the air. "I was using poetic license to make a point. This mystery man must be something special. Please tell me he has a brother. I'm currently in a bit of a dry spell myself."

"He does," Abby said. "But unfortunately for you, he's already married."

"Bummer."

"Yeah." Abby debated how much to say. If she admitted the full extent of how meeting Duncan Stewart had affected her, Lara would never let it go. "Do you know Isobel Stewart?"

"Of course. Everyone knows Miss Izzy. She has several accounts at the bank."

Lara was a loan officer at the local financial institution, a position with a great deal of responsibility and authority in a small town. She, like Abby, found Candlewick's pool of eligible men to be lamentably small. Not only that, but a lot of guys were put off by Lara's cool demeanor and elegant looks. Abby's friend had the proverbial heart of gold, but she had been known to freeze a man in his tracks if he stepped over an invisible line.

"Well, this was Miss Izzy's grandson."

"Brody?"

"No. He's the one who just got married."

"To the bookstore lady…"

"Right."

"So there's a brother number two?"

"Oh, yeah."

"It's the accent, isn't it? I'll bet even if he had two heads and warts, women would fall all over him."

"Are you saying I'm shallow?"

"Don't be defensive. Tell me why he's so adorable and irresistible that my dearest friend is in a dither."

"I don't even know what that means."

"A dither. A state of flustered excitement or fear."

Well, poop. That was Abby's exact state. "There was something about him, Lara. An intensity. Or maybe an air of danger. I'm not sure I can explain it. He was very *masculine*."

Lara's eyes rounded. She fanned herself with her napkin and took a sip of water. "So what are we going to do to make sure this very dangerously masculine man notices you?"

Abby tried not to smirk. "Not really an issue. He's already asked me out."

Her friend with the runway-model body and the ash-blond hair and the sapphire eyes goggled. "Seriously? It was the boobs, wasn't it? Lord, what I wouldn't give to have those boobs for twenty-four hours. They're guy magnets."

"I don't think he was even serious," Abby admitted, voicing her worst fears. "He's lonely, and by his own admission, he doesn't know anybody in town."

"There must have been more to it than that or you wouldn't be acting so jittery."

Abby's cheeks flamed hotter. "He flirted with me

almost from the beginning, and then he asked me out. But he also insulted my profession and questioned my motives. I didn't know what to say."

"So what *did* you say?"

"I told him I had to think about it."

"Ah. That's good. Make him work for it."

"Lara! That's not what I meant. I'm not sure my dating him is ethical. I've worked too hard to get where I am in my career…to make sure everyone knows that I'm not like my father."

"Oh, good grief. You're not representing him in a court of law. Besides, isn't Miss Izzy technically your *boss's* client?"

"Yes, but—"

Lara interrupted with a triumphant grin. "Problem solved. Now for the important question. Do you have any good undies, and what are you going to wear when you finally put him out of his misery?"

Two

Abby chose to wait a week before contacting Duncan Stewart. That would give her time to decide if she really wanted to go out with him. If she realized in the interim that he had only been playing with her, then she wouldn't have embarrassed herself for nothing.

She planned to call him the following Saturday morning. The Friday night before, Lara was at her house for a battle-of-the-Chrises movie night. It was an old game they played. Tonight would be Chris Pine versus Chris Hemsworth.

While they popped popcorn in the kitchen, Lara rummaged in the fridge. "Has your dad harassed you lately?" she asked, popping the tab on a soda and taking a sip before hopping up on the butcher block countertop and dangling her legs.

Abby grimaced. "No, thank God. He's been suspiciously quiet. Almost too quiet. Makes me nervous."

"Mom wanted me to make sure you know you're invited to our place for Thanksgiving."

"That's a long time from now," Abby said, her throat tight.

"Not all that long. My mom loves you. Our whole family loves you. It's not your fault that your father has gone off the deep end."

Abby dumped the popcorn into two bowls and sighed. "It feels like my fault. Maybe I should have tried harder to get him medical help. I don't know if he has diagnosable medical issues or if he's just a deeply disturbed jerk."

"I shouldn't have brought it up," Lara said, her expression rueful. "But I can't bear to see you go through the holidays again like you did last year. That was hell. You're like my sister, Abbs. And you deserve better." She hopped down and grabbed a bowl. "Enough gloomy talk. Let's eat. Don't forget the cheesecake I brought."

"Do cheesecake and popcorn really go together?"

"Cheesecake goes with everything," Lara said.

An hour and a half later, when the first movie credits rolled, Abby was already yawning. "Sorry," she muttered. "I didn't sleep much last night."

Lara kicked her foot. "Dreaming about the luscious Scotsman?"

"Not exactly. He hasn't contacted me, you know."

"If I'm not mistaken, you told him to give you time to think about it."

"I did."

"So what's the problem?"

"I don't know if I want to go out with him."

"Liar."

"Excuse me!" Abby said, affronted.

"Of course you *want* to go out with him. But you're scared."

"Oh." That much was true. "I'm fifteen pounds overweight, Lara."

"Not every guy wants a stick figure. He liked what he saw. And besides, you're a beautiful woman, whether you believe it or not."

Easy for Lara to say. She was the epitome of the perfect female. If she weren't so wonderful, Abby would be compelled to hate her on sight. "Well, it's a moot point, because he hasn't gotten back to me, and I honestly don't think I have the guts to call him."

"Let's look at this objectively, honey. How often do new men wander into town?"

"Almost never."

"And when they do, how often are they young, hot and available?"

"Almost never."

"And when one of them is young, hot and available, how often is he the decent type who loves his grandma and is willing to sacrifice his own happiness for hers?"

"You're making him sound like a cross between Robin Hood and James Bond. I'm pretty sure Duncan Stewart just wants to get laid."

"That's what all men want. It wouldn't hurt you either."

"Lara!"

"You're staring down the barrel at thirty. Then it'll be thirty-five and forty. All the good men will be gone. You've got a live one on the hook, Abby. Don't toss him back."

"That's the most sexually regressive, ridiculous speech I've ever heard."

"You know I'm right."

"I don't see you *fishing*."

"Maybe if I had a charming Scotsman asking me out, I would be."

"I don't know. He's arrogant and rich and snarky. Probably hasn't had to work for anything in his life."

"Text him. Right now. Tell him yes."

"You're bullying me."

"Correction. I'm *encouraging* you. There's a difference."

Abby picked up her cell phone, her stomach churning. "I don't know what to say."

"Do it, Abby."

Without warning, her cell phone dinged. She was so startled, she almost dropped it. The words on the screen left no doubt about the sender.

Have I given ye enough time, lass? Dinner Tuesday? Pick you up at 6?

"It's him, Lara." She held out the phone. "He must have been serious."

Lara read the text and beamed. "Of course he was serious. The man has good taste. Text him back. Hurry."

Hands shaking, Abby pecked out a reply...

Two conditions. We don't call it a date. And you let

me tell you about the offer on your grandmother's business…

She hit Send and sighed. "I'm not finishing the rest of that dessert. Do you think I can lose ten pounds by Tuesday?"

Lara handed her a fork. "Eat the damn cheesecake. You're perfect just the way you are. If Duncan Stewart doesn't agree, he's an idiot."

Duncan had fallen into a routine of sorts. It wasn't familiar, and it wasn't home, but for the moment, it was workable. His grandmother liked to sleep later in her old age. Since Duncan was up early every day, he headed into town and opened up the office before anyone else arrived. He liked having a chance to look over things unobserved.

He was definitely the new kid on the block. All the staff had been cordial and helpful, but he guessed they were wondering if anyone would be getting the ax. That wasn't his plan at all. Stewart Properties appeared to be thriving. It was up to him to make sure that success continued.

The company comprised two equally profitable arms—mountain cabin construction and mountain cabin rentals. Isobel and Geoffrey had capitalized on a tourist market in its infancy decades ago, and had built their reputation bit by bit. The main office had been located in Candlewick since the beginning, but satellite offices operated in Asheville and several other spots within a hundred-mile radius.

In a little over a week's time, Duncan had learned the basics of daily operations. He had already spotted the invaluable employees and the ones who might be potential problems. Because his training and degrees were in finance, he wasn't concerned about the accounting practices. Where he would have to pay attention was in the actual design and building modules.

Because his grandmother was determined to maintain her involvement in the day-to-day operations, he went back up the mountain each morning around eleven and picked her up at the palatial wood-and-stone home she and her husband had built for themselves. It was far too big for an elderly widow. It was even too big with Duncan in the house. But Isobel wanted to stay, so the status quo remained.

After a shared lunch in town, Duncan deferred to Isobel's decisions and insights about the various company decisions. Her mind was as sharp as it ever had been. Her stamina, however, was less reliable. Some days, she made it until closing time at five. Other times, someone was drafted to take her home at three.

This particular Tuesday was a good day. Duncan and Isobel had spent several hours going over potential new architectural plans for a series of cabins to be built on land they had recently acquired. Other, somewhat dated, house plans were being culled.

At last, Isobel closed the final folder and tapped it with a gnarled finger. "These new ones are going to be very popular. You mark my words."

Duncan scrubbed his hands across his scalp and yawned, standing up when she did. "I believe you, Granny. You're the boss."

Isobel reached for his hand and pressed it to her cheek. "Thank you, my boy. Thank you for everything you've done for an old woman. It means more to me than you'll ever know."

He hugged her, glad she couldn't see how much he had struggled with the decision to uproot his life. "I love you, Granny. You looked after Brody and me when we were lost boys after Mom and Dad divorced. I owe you for that, even if for nothing else. Besides, I'm enjoying myself."

And it was true. He was. He hadn't expected to, not at all, so the rush of adrenaline in the midst of new challenges was a bonus.

When they released each other and stepped back, he grinned. "I suppose I should tell you. I have a date tonight. Don't wait up for me."

The old woman's eyes sparkled, and she chortled with glee. "Do tell, boy. Anybody I know?"

"Abby Hartmann? She's at the law firm where you sent me to sign the new will."

"Ah, yes. Abby." Isobel's brows narrowed. "Abby is a nice young woman."

"Why do I get the impression you don't approve?"

"Abby hasn't had an easy life. She deserves to be treated well."

"I wasna' planning on beating her, Granny."

"Don't be sassy, boy. You know what I mean. I'd not want you to trifle with her affections."

"She strikes me as an extremely savvy young woman. I think she can handle herself."

"Maybe so. Will you bring her by the house so I can say hello?"

"Next time perhaps. Let's see how tonight goes."

Isobel's eyes gleamed. "So you're not entirely sure of yourself. That's a good thing."

"Whose side are you on?" he complained.

"I'll always be in your corner, Duncan, but we women have to stick together."

Several hours later, Duncan parked in front of Abby's neat, bungalow-style white frame house and studied the property. She lived on a quiet side street only two blocks off the town square. Her handkerchief-sized yard was neatly manicured, and her windows gleamed in the early evening sun.

Since the moment Abby accepted his invitation Friday night, they had texted back and forth a time or two. He found himself eager to see her again, surprisingly so. Perhaps he needed a break from work or a distraction from his complicated new life. Or maybe he simply wanted to determine if the gut-level attraction he experienced in her office was still there.

Her conditions for accepting his invitation had angered him at first. But after some consideration, he decided, what the hell? Abby could talk about this mystery buyer all she wanted. It wasn't going to change the bottom line.

When she opened the door at his knock, he caught his breath. Her smile was tentative, but everything else about her was no-holds-barred. The glorious hair. Her long-sleeved hunter green silk dress that hugged her hourglass figure from shoulders to knees. Black stiletto heels that gave her an additional few inches of height.

"You look beautiful," he said gruffly. "I'm very glad you decided to say yes."

"Me, too. Let me grab my purse."

They chatted about inconsequential topics on the drive to Claremont, both of them on their best behavior. The drive was just long enough to break the ice. Duncan had chosen an upscale special-occasion restaurant that specialized in French cuisine.

When he helped Abby out of the car, his hand beneath her elbow, the punch of desire left him breathless. He'd been celibate out of necessity during this transition from Scotland to North Carolina, but whatever he felt for the petite lawyer was more than a sexual dry spell. She fascinated him.

Over dinner, he quizzed her about her life. "So tell me about your childhood. Did you always want to be a lawyer? I thought most girls went the princess route at first."

Abby laughed as he had wanted her to. Her long-lashed eyes reminded him of a kitten he'd had as a boy. He'd named her Smoke, and she had followed him everywhere.

The waiter interrupted momentarily. Afterward, Abby answered his question. "To be honest, I was obsessed with the idea of international studies. I wanted to go to college abroad, anything to get away from my hometown. But I was pragmatic, even as a kid. I knew we didn't have the finances to swing that. My mom died when I was three, so my dad raised me on his own. Money was always tight."

"Law school isn't cheap."

"No. I was very lucky. Mr. Chester Sr., who was your grandparents' original lawyer, had a long-standing tradition of mentoring students at the local high school. When he died, his son continued the program. I was fortunate enough to get an internship at the law firm during my senior year in high school. I realized that I liked the work. After four years at a state university,

Mr. Chester helped me with law school applications, and I was accepted at Wake Forest. When I finished, they offered me a job here in Candlewick."

"Didn't you have aspirations to head for the big city and make your mark?"

Abby's smile slipped. He couldn't quite read her expression. "I think we all imagine what it would be like to start over someplace new. For me, the pluses of staying put outweighed any negatives. I haven't regretted my decisions. How about you, Duncan? What was your life like back in Scotland?"

He shrugged, even now feeling the bittersweet pull of all he had left behind. "Ye've heard of the Isle of Skye, I suppose. It's truly as beautiful as they say. Water and sky and everything in between."

"You miss it. I hear it in your voice."

"Aye. But I'm a grown man. I can handle a bit of disappointment."

"How did you wind up working with your brother?"

"Brody started the boating business, both commercial fishing and tourist craft, when he was in his twenties. When I finished university, he begged me to join him and handle the financial stuff. We've had a good partnership over the years."

"You told me that day in my office that he's holding the job for you."

"He wants to. I don't think it makes sense. Granny is healthy as a horse. She could live for another decade. And I hope she does."

He was shocked when Abby smiled at him and reached across the table to take one of his hands in hers. Her fingers were soft and warm. "I think you're a very sweet man, Duncan Stewart."

"I'm *not* sweet." He bristled.

She stroked her thumb across his knuckles. "It's a compliment."

"Didn't sound like one." He lifted his free hand, the one Abby wasn't holding, and summoned the waitress. "May we see a dessert menu, please?"

"Oh, not for me," Abby said, her smile dimming.

"They're famous for their bread pudding. I read about it on Yelp."

"You'll have to eat it. I'm too full."

"Nonsense. You only had a salad and a tiny chicken breast. I can't eat dessert alone."

Now Abby looked genuinely upset. She let go of his hand, leaving him bereft. "No dessert," she said firmly. "I'm dieting."

He ordered one for himself anyway and frowned. "Why in God's name are you dieting, lass? You're perfect."

Abby stared at him, waiting for the punch line... searching for the calculation in his eyes, the attempt to butter her up with compliments to lure her into bed. She saw none of that. Instead, Duncan seemed genuinely baffled and irritated by her insistence on refusing dessert.

She tried again. "You're tall and lean, Duncan. For women like me who are short and chu—"

He reached across the table and put his hand over her mouth. "Don't you dare say it. My God, girl. Are the men in this country blind and stupid? I've spent every minute of this evening wondering how long it will be until I get to see your naked curvy body pressed up against mine. And you're worried about dessert?"

The waitress arrived with a decadent bread pudding topped off with real whipped cream. She set the plate on the table with fresh napkins and two spoons and walked away. In the ensuing silence, Abby felt her face turn red. Embarrassment mixed with sexual tension.

Duncan, his expression inscrutable, picked up a spoon and scooped out a bite of caramel-laced, whipped-cream-topped perfection. "Open your mouth, lass. I've an urge to feed you, since I can't do anything else at the moment."

Abby's lips parted even as her knees pressed together. The way Duncan Stewart was looking at her ought to be illegal.

He lifted the spoon to her mouth. "Wider," he said hoarsely.

She obeyed and moaned when he spooned the dessert between her lips. The flavors exploded onto her tongue. She chewed and swallowed, light-headed. Duncan watched her like a hungry hawk studying a mouse. "Do you like it?" he asked. His voice was sandpaper, the accent almost buried beneath rough desire.

"Yes." The word stuck in her throat. "Do you want some?"

"Only if you feed it to me."

Abby recognized the sexual challenge for what it was. Never in her life had she found herself in such a position. Duncan Stewart had turned a simple meal into sexual foreplay, and now he demanded an equal partner.

"I don't sleep with a man on the first date," she said desperately, reminding herself of all the reasons she made that rule.

"Understood. Besides, this isn't a date—remember?" He growled his response, restless, agitated. "I'll settle for dessert. Now, lass. Before it gets cold."

The way Abby felt, she was never going to be cold again. With trembling fingers, she retrieved the spoon and scooped a bite for Duncan. He watched her intently.

"Stop that," she complained.

"Stop what?" His complacent smile was suspect.

"Stop imagining me naked."

"Is that what I was doing? I didn't know you were a mind reader."

"Open your mouth, Duncan."

"Yes, ma'am."

Why had she never realized how erotic it could be to feed a man dessert? When Duncan's sharp white teeth barely missed her finger as he snagged the pudding, she shuddered. "Is that enough?" She sat back in her chair and took a hasty drink of water, almost choking.

The man laughed at her, damn him.

"I'm still hungry," he said.

"Feed yourself."

"If you're not going to sleep with me tonight, I thought we could at least sublimate."

"Do they teach you that line in wicked, sexy Scotsman school?"

Three

Duncan chuckled, though his sex was hard as stone and he wanted to howl at the notion he couldn't have her tonight. "I have no idea. I've no' been particularly successful with the ladies over the years. Too busy with work, I suppose."

"Oh, please."

"'Tis true," he insisted. "There haven't been as many women as you might think. Brody was always the one with the easy banter and the sunny personality. I spent a lot of time alone. I liked walking the moors and tinkering with boat engines and whatnot. Women were complicated and sometimes, frankly, too much work."

"So why me?"

At first he thought she was flirting, begging for a compliment. But on second glance, he saw the uncertainty beneath the question, and it squeezed his heart. "Ah, heavens, Abby, ye're poetry wrapped in a woman's body. I walked into your office and it was like being punched in the chest. I could have taken you then and there. I can't explain it. Perhaps you think I'm daft."

She stared at him, eyes huge. She gnawed her bottom lip. "It's not natural for a man your age to have to live with his grandmother. You're a long way from where you belong. I think you're probably homesick and horny. It's skewed your thinking. I've never driven *anyone* sexually insane."

"Surely you've heard of chemistry, sweet lass."

The doubt on her face made him determined to tamp down his own lust until he could convince her of his sincerity.

"Is that what this is?" she asked.

"Maybe. Or a bit of fairy magic. We Scots are staunch believers in fairies, you know."

Abby smiled wryly. "Here's the thing, Duncan. I like you. Mostly. And let's be honest. You're a very sexy, appealing man. But this sounds like a really bad idea."

"Why is that?"

"If we end up in bed together, I risk becoming the latest gossipy tidbit in Candlewick. I've worked too hard to prove myself in a career that's extremely important to me."

"So we'll fly under the radar. Secret love affairs can be very hot."

"I think you're missing the point," she sputtered, mortification painting her cheeks crimson.

"I know what I want, Abby. If you're honest, I

think you want it, too." Her resistance made him push all the harder. "But if I'm wrong, all you have to do is say no, and I'll leave you alone."

The long silence that followed made him regret his noble pronouncement.

At last, Abby spoke, her expression troubled. "If we do this, you and I would definitely be temporary. Short and secret would be the name of the game. I don't want the whole world to know when it's over. So if they never know when it starts, we dodge that issue."

Some of his jubilant mood faded. "I've never gone into a relationship already planning its demise," he groused.

"Lawyers are all about endings and beginnings. It's what we do. Life flows more smoothly when expectations are clear and everyone signs on the dotted line, metaphorically speaking, of course."

He pretended to wipe his brow. "Whew. I thought you were about to make me sign a contract before I undress you."

"I thought about it," she said.

"You're joking." He raised an eyebrow, searching her features for the truth.

Abby's grimace was self-mocking. "You know… lights out. Nothing too kinky at first."

"Define *at first*."

He was delighted when her choked laughter told him she understood his naughty question.

Abby glanced at her watch. "This has been lovely, but I *do* have work tomorrow."

"Of course." He paid the check, and they made their way to the car. Though it was only early September, in the mountains, the nights cooled rapidly after the sun went down.

His companion was quiet…too quiet. He would give a lot to know what she was thinking. She hadn't once mentioned the prospective buyer for Stewart Properties. He was relieved, but the omission worried him. He hated secrets. Did the sexy lawyer have some wicked plan in mind to wait until he was weak with wanting and then try to coerce him into selling? He didn't know her well enough to trust her.

It wasn't hubris on his part to believe he could coax her into bed tonight if he pressed the issue. Sexual arousal hummed between them like a breathless, tangible force, incubated and nourished by circumstance. The faint scent of feminine perfume in the air. Her slightly off-key humming to the songs on the radio. The pair of sexy high heels that tumbled to the floor of the car when Abby kicked them off and curled her legs beneath her for the ride back to Candlewick.

Duncan gripped the steering wheel, white-knuckled. The road home was strewn with dark, convenient pull-offs where a man could drag a woman against him and undress her and dive deep to slake his hunger.

He wanted Abby with a wild, urgent passion that rattled him and made him restless. His own reckless urges gave him pause. She asked for time. Time would be his friend. All he had to do was cultivate a modicum of patience.

God help him, perhaps he could do it.

On Abby's front porch, he curled an arm around her waist and eased her into the shadows for a good-night kiss. She made no pretense of protest.

As kisses went, it was world-class. They jumped

straight over *getting to know you* and ploughed into *where have you been all my life?* Abby was short and he was tall, so the logistics were tricky. Abby solved their dilemma by hopping up onto the door stoop.

Now he could run his hands from her shoulders to her narrow waist to the sensational curves of her bottom. The thin fabric of her green silky dress was no barrier at all. "Ye're a stunning woman, Abby Hartmann," he muttered. "I'm glad we met." He nipped the side of her neck with his teeth and grinned when she made a little squeak in the back of her throat and nuzzled closer.

"Me, too," she said. "Thank you for dinner."

"So polite," he teased.

"It's what we do here in the South. But don't mistake nice manners for being a pushover."

"Understood." He had never felt such an odd mixture of lust and tenderness toward a woman. "I'll feed you again tomorrow night," he said. "Six still work?"

Abby pulled back and ran her hands through her hair, visibly flustered, even in the semidarkness. Her porch light was off, but the streetlight out at the road gave them a hint of illumination. "I have book club tomorrow night," she said. She rummaged in her small purse, extracted a key and unlocked the door.

"Thursday?"

"Dinner with friends."

He ground his teeth until his jaw ached. "Friday?"

She turned, linked her arms around his neck and kissed him square on the mouth, her magnificent breasts pressed firmly against his chest. "Friday would be perfect. But only if you take me by the house to see your grandmother beforehand and let me tell her about the buyer Mr. Chester has in the wings."

Duncan lost it for a good ninety seconds, maybe a full two minutes. He forgot where he was. He forgot he had decided to be a gentleman. He even forgot he was in a semipublic setting.

He was angry and aroused, a dangerous combo. Abby's lips were addictive. She looked so charming and innocent in person, but she tasted like sin. He wanted to strip her bare and take her up against the front door. Her hands played restlessly with his belt at the back of his waist. His erection was buried in the softness of her stomach. There was no hiding the state of his body. She had to know.

But she didn't back away, and she didn't seem to mind.

At last, and to his eternal embarrassment, Abby was the one to drag them back from the edge. "I have to go inside, Duncan."

She said it apologetically, stroking his cheek with one hand as if she could pacify the raging beast inside him.

He shuddered and dragged in a great lungful of air in an attempt to find control. "Of course." He stole one last, hurried kiss. At least he meant it to be hurried. In the end, he lingered, coaxing her lips apart with the tip of his tongue and stroking the inside of her mouth until they both breathed raggedly.

Finally, he cupped her face in his hands and kissed her nose. "Stop seducing me, woman."

"I'm not," she protested.

He dared to cup one of her breasts through two layers of smooth cloth. The weight of her firm, rounded flesh nestled in his palm. The pert, firm nipple begged for the touch of his thumb. "Aye, lass," he said. "Aye, ye are."

Abby escaped into the house with her virtue intact, but it was a close call. She slammed the door, locked it and peered through the curtains to make sure the tall, handsome Scotsman made his way back to his car.

Her knees trembled and her mouth was dry. She was such a fraud. From the beginning, she had known that going out with Duncan Stewart was a bad idea. She had rationalized to herself that getting on good terms with him could mean an opportunity to press the case for selling his grandmother's business.

And yet as the evening unfolded, Abby had let herself be sidetracked by the warmth of the Scotsman's wicked smile. This was exactly the kind of thing that made mixing business with pleasure problematic. She was supposed to be initiating contact with Duncan's grandmother and explaining why selling Stewart Properties could be in Miss Isobel's best interests. Instead, Abby had forgotten her mission, endangered her stellar reputation in the law office and danced perilously close to becoming Duncan's temporary fling.

The following day on her lunch hour, she and Lara munched apples and did their customary two-mile walk. Lara, being Lara, didn't bother to hide her eagerness for details. "Spill it, Abby. Give me every juicy tidbit. My vicarious love life is all I have at the moment."

Abby swallowed the last bite of fruit and tossed the

core in a public trash receptacle as they rounded the corner and headed away from downtown. "I had fun."

"That's it?"

"He's interesting...well traveled, well-read. A gentleman."

"Well, that sounds boring as hell."

"No, it doesn't. You're just being mean. It was nice to spend time with a man who can carry on a conversation." She didn't mention the whole dessert thing. Even now she couldn't think about the bread pudding incident without getting aroused and flustered.

"So no sex?" Lara eyed her with an expression that was equal parts resignation and disappointment.

They finished the third circuit of the block and turned back toward their respective places of employment. "You know me, Lara. I'm not impulsive, especially when it comes to intimacy."

"You went out with a client. That's a start."

Abby stopped in the middle of the sidewalk, her heart pumping, and stared at her friend. "I thought you said my dating him was okay?"

Lara's smile was smug. "It's not up to me, now is it? At least tell me he kissed you good night."

Abby shoved her hands in the pockets of her black dress pants and started walking again. "Yes. So?"

"Are we talking a polite peck on the cheek?"

"Not exactly."

"You're such a tease."

Lara grabbed her arm, but Abby evaded the hold and kept walking. "I have an appointment in fifteen minutes. Gotta get back."

"Well, shoot." Lara glanced at her watch and realized what time it was. "This conversation isn't over."

She raised her voice to be heard as Abby headed in the opposite direction.

Abby gave her a wave over the shoulder. "See you tonight."

Fortunately for Abby, Lara was more circumspect during their once-a-month book club meeting that evening. The dozen women in the group ranged in age from Lara and Abby's twenty-something to eighty-one. This week, they were meeting in a back room at the pizza shop.

Over cheesy slices of thick-crust pepperoni, the conversation zipped and zinged from one topic to the next before settling on the plot of the novel they were supposed to have read. Abby had finished most of it. The heroine died of a terrible disease two chapters from the end, so she had lost interest.

Lara loved stirring up controversy and discussion. While Abby's friend debated whether or not the hero's character was supposed to symbolize lost dreams, Abby surreptitiously fished her cell phone from her purse and checked for messages. She hadn't heard a peep from Duncan since he left her last night. Maybe her insistence on talking to Miss Izzy had scared him off.

He seemed pretty mad when she suggested it, but then again, not so mad that he hadn't kissed her until her toes curled and her limbs turned to water. The man knew how to kiss.

If he'd changed his mind about the second date, it was probably a good thing.

When the waitress came to do drink refills, Lara lowered her voice and leaned in. "Whatcha doin', kiddo? This is supposed to be a work-free zone."

"It's not work," Abby said. "I was only checking to see if I had a text from Duncan. He asked me out again for Friday night, but I made him mad, so he may be done with me."

"What did you do that was so terrible?"

"I told him I would only go out with him a second time if he would take me to see Miss Izzy beforehand and let me tell her about the offer we have for her property."

Lara sat back in her seat and pursed her lips. The conversation ebbed and flowed around them. "I'm impressed. Playing hardball."

"It's not that," Abby whispered. "But Mr. Chester asked me to take care of *one* thing while he's on leave, one simple thing. All I need to do is tell Miss Izzy about the offer. If she's really dead set against selling, all she has to do is say no. I will have fulfilled my obligation, and that will be the end of it. I don't know why Duncan is making such a big deal about it."

"I'll bet *I* do."

"How could you possibly know what that Scotsman is thinking?"

"He didn't really want to move here, right?"

"Correct."

"And if Miss Izzy accepts the offer being brokered by your law firm, Stewart Properties changes hands and Duncan is off the hook. The poor man probably feels guilty, because deep down, he *wants* you to convince his grandmother to sell out. But that makes him a bad person, so it's easier to keep you away from her."

"Well, it's a moot point because I don't think his dinner invitation is still on the table."

Lara reached for a breadstick and dunked it in homemade marinara sauce. "The man wants you, Abby. He'll figure out a way to have you and appease his conscience at the same time. You wait and see."

Four

By Thursday evening, Abby's spirits hit rock bottom, and her opinion of Lara's romantic advice fell lower still. Forty-eight hours had passed and not a single word from Duncan Stewart. The man kissed her as if she had been the only oasis in a trackless desert, and then he had simply walked away.

She almost opted out of dinner with friends. It was difficult to fake a good mood when all she wanted to do was watch romantic comedies and mope around her small house. In the end, she went, but only because the outing took her mind off Duncan and the affair that never was.

No matter how many times she told herself it was for the best—that it was completely inappropriate for her to date the grandson of one of Mr. Chester's influential clients—she didn't believe it in her heart.

How long had it been since a man was really interested her? Almost never?

Duncan Stewart might ruin her for other men, but that was a risk she was prepared to take. Even knowing he would be in Candlewick a limited amount of time, maybe only two years (and that their affair would likely be far shorter than that), was not a negative.

He fascinated her. For once in her neatly planned life, she wanted to make the rash, dangerous choice. She wanted Duncan.

When dinner wound to an end, she decided to leave her car at the restaurant and walk the relatively short distance home. She'd had several glasses of wine, so she didn't want to take any chances that she might not be in full control. The night was crisp with a hint of autumn, but not cold. Other people were out and about on the streets even at this hour.

Crime was virtually nonexistent in Candlewick. Some people compared their little town to the fictional Mayberry. In many cases, that description wasn't far off.

By the time she made it to her street and up the block to her own sidewalk, it was late. Sleepy, and still caught up in wondering about Duncan, she didn't spot the intruder at first. Then something moved in the shadows, and she sucked in a sharp breath.

Frozen with fear and in quick succession disgust, she called out to the shadowy figure. "What are you doing here, Daddy?" She stayed where she was out at the road, not wanting him to follow her into the house.

The large hulking shadow turned into an old man under the harsh glare of the streetlight. Once upon a time her father had been handsome and dapper. Even now—when he wanted to—he could clean himself up, get a haircut and present to the world a reasonable facsimile of a sophisticated adult.

Unfortunately, his demons—both mental and pharmaceutical—now controlled him to such a degree that most days he was a broken-down shamble of a man.

"I wanted to see my baby, but I couldn't get in the house," he said. The words were slurred. When he moved closer, she smelled alcohol on his breath.

Abby clutched her purse more tightly in her arms. "Well, you've seen me. I need to get to bed. It's late." She took a breath. "The reason you couldn't get in is because I changed all my locks."

He held out his hand, his expression half cagey, half pitiful. "You're doin' mighty well in that lawyer job of yours. How 'bout giving your old man a loan? I'm running a little short this month."

Don't engage. Don't engage. Don't engage. The mantra had preserved her emotional health and sanity on more than one occasion. "I have to go," she said. No matter how unfounded, waves of guilt battered her self-esteem. It was not even the middle of the month. He received several pension checks, one from the government and a couple of others from his few stable periods of employment. There was no reason in the world for him to be out of money.

Even if he was, it wasn't her responsibility. She turned her back on him and took a step. But Howard Lander was not giving up.

He scuttled up beside her. "A hundred, Abby girl. That's all. And I'll pay you back, I swear."

Fury rose inside her chest in a choking cloud. Good parents provided a loving, nurturing environment for their children to succeed. Not only did Abby's father not support her as a teen and young adult, he had actually harmed her and nearly derailed her academic successes.

"If you don't stay away from me," she said, her throat raw with tears, "I'm going to take out a restraining order against you."

The old man stumbled and gaped, genuine puzzlement in his half-vacant expression. "Why would you say that?"

Abby laughed, though she wanted to sob. "Every time you come inside my house, you steal from me, Dad. Money, jewelry, prescription drugs. Did you somehow think I never noticed?"

Even in his addled state, he didn't bother to deny her accusation. "I've had a few hard times. No reason for a man's daughter to be cold and cruel."

"I can't do this anymore, Daddy. If you won't leave me alone, I swear I'll move to the other side of the country. It's embarrassing enough that the whole town knows what kind of man you are."

He'd been a door-to-door salesman back when that was still a thing. A combination of charm and dogged persistence had given him moderate success. In between bouts of selling encyclopedias and household items, he'd chased one get-rich-quick scheme after another, always convinced that his fortune was just around the next corner.

By the time Abby was eight, Howard Lander stopped *wasting* his money on babysitters, instead choosing to leave her at home alone after school and on the weekends. Fortunately, she had been mature for her age and not prone to wild stunts that might have endangered her life or burned down their home.

For Abby, high school graduation brought a moment of release, of freedom. College and grad school had been some of the happiest years of her life. Coming home to Candlewick and working for the Chesters' law firm, on the other hand, had been a mixed blessing.

Her father stood, shoulders hunched, staring at the ground. "I never meant to harm anyone. I've made my share of mistakes, but I had good intentions."

Sadly, that part was probably true. There was no malice in the old man. Only unfounded optimism, a total misunderstanding of finances and an ability to con people out of their money one way or another.

"Good night." Abby made herself walk away, but her father was in one of his more stubborn moods, fueled by alcoholic courage.

"You owe me," he shouted. "I could have given you up for adoption when your mother died, but I didn't. That's worth something. Wouldn't look too good for you if I start telling everyone how badly you treat the only parent you've ever known."

The callous, calculating threat put another crack in her shattered heart. She had paid for her meal that night with cash. The change was in her pocket. Seven dollars and thirty-two cents. She fished it out and shoved it at him. "Take it and go. I don't want to see you here ever again."

She ran up the walk and into the house, slamming the door and bolting it behind her. The tears came in earnest, blurring her vision and knotting her stomach. The bedroom was too far. She fell onto the sofa, buried her face in the cushions and cried until her bones ached.

Every time she tangled with her father now, she felt dirty. She had worked so hard to make something of herself...to lead a decent, normal life. Yet always, her past hung over her head, reminding her that she might forever be tainted by his dishonesty.

At ten, she dragged herself down the hall to take a shower. Looking in the mirror was a mistake. Her eyes were bloodshot and puffy, and smeared mascara made her resemble a rabid panda. It was a good thing Duncan Stewart couldn't see her now.

As if she had summoned him somehow with her thoughts, her phone dinged. She picked it up and read the text.

We never made a plan for tomorrow night, did we?

They hadn't. She had agreed to see him again only if she could speak with Miss Izzy first about the prospective buyer. She gripped the phone, torn about how to answer. She knew that dating Duncan Stewart was a dead end and a bad idea. Ethics aside, they had nothing in common. He was wealthy and had lived a life of relative ease.

She was sure he'd never had to worry about having the electricity or the water turned off because the bills hadn't been paid in three months. And she was equally positive he had never been forced to eat boxed macaroni and cheese five nights in a row because it was the only thing in the pantry a kid could microwave easily. Or the only food available, period.

Wistfully, she did the grown-up thing.

I don't think it's a good idea for us to see each other socially, Duncan. Too many layers of complications.

Thirty seconds passed. Then sixty. At last, the phone dinged.

What about that kiss?

Despite her low mood, she smiled.

What about it?

Don't be coy, Abby. We're both adults. I want you. You want me.

She tried to be incensed by his careless arrogance, but damn it, the man was right.

Not all itches have to be scratched.

You don't know me very well yet, but here's the thing, lass. I rarely take no for an answer.

Neither do I! She threw in a few emojis for good measure.

Fine. I'll take you to see Granny before dinner. But don't be surprised when she says no to your buyer.

And if she says yes????

Abby could almost *feel* the frustrated male silence on the other end. Maybe Lara was right. Maybe Duncan was conflicted about letting Abby get to his grandmother, because if the offer was good enough, he'd be off the hook and headed home to Scotland.

At last, he answered. I'll pick you up at five thirty. We'll have hors d'oeuvres with her, and you can make your pitch. But no bullying or hard-sell tactics. If she says no, you drop the subject. Period.

You're an arrogant ass, Duncan Stewart.

Aye, but you like me anyway…

She turned off the phone and tossed it in a drawer, as if it had the power to regenerate and bite her.

Duncan was dangerous to her peace of mind for many reasons. Clearly, he knew women well enough to recognize mutual interest when he witnessed it. Abby could protest 'til the cows came home that this relationship was a terrible idea. All Duncan had to do was kiss her until she forgot the many reasons why she should stay away from him.

Friday was an exercise in torture for Duncan. Every time he saw his granny's smiling face, he felt guilty. Tonight, he was going to let a lawyer with her own nest-feathering agenda get close to his grandmother, just so he could find his way into that lawyer's bed.

Any way you sliced it, that made him scum.

In the moments when he wasn't thinking about Abby, he pondered the escape clause in the will. He had come here to America, fully expecting his grandmother to live for another decade or more. It was possible. The women in her genealogy had all closed in on the centennial mark, several of them passing it. Granny Isobel could very well celebrate her hundredth birthday here in Candlewick. She was in good health and of sound mind.

To hear that his indenture had an escape clause troubled him. Without it, he had no choice but to dive headfirst into Stewart Properties and make a new life for himself. But knowing there was a carrot dangling out there—the chance to go home to Scotland in two years—meant that he would always be marking time. In many ways, the possibility of reprieve made things worse.

In a difficult situation, a man needed to hunker down and make the best of his fate. How effective would Duncan be if he were always looking wistfully over his shoulder from whence he had come?

Somehow, he made it through the day. Granny Isobel was beside herself at the prospect of company. She had ordered a trio of fancy appetizers from a local caterer, along with a selection of wines to have on hand for Abby's visit.

One of the receptionists took Isobel home at three so she could nap in preparation for her visitor. Duncan stayed at the office until the very last minute, going over spreadsheets and trying his damnedest to wrap his head around the ambitious construction schedule planned for the upcoming two quarters.

The business's forward motion had slowed in the year since his grandfather's death. First Brody, and now Duncan, had helped Isobel get the company back on track. It relieved Duncan more than a little to know that auditors would be coming in soon. If there were any problems, he wanted to know about them.

At five, he called his grandmother to see if she needed anything else to go with the food. She professed to have it all under control. He grinned to himself. In his grandparents' heyday, they had thrown wildly lavish parties up on top of the mountain. Invitations to the big house were highly coveted. He'd heard more than one story about dancing until dawn and draining multiple cases of champagne and good Scottish whisky.

At five twenty, he locked up the office and headed out to pick up Abby.

When he bounded up her steps and knocked, she answered the door wearing a smile, black dress pants and a soft berry-pink cashmere sweater that clung to her ample curves. He scooped her up and kissed her, careful not to smudge her rosy lip gloss.

Abby was stiff in his embrace at first, but then she sighed and kissed him back. "You're an outrageous man. I don't know why I don't smack you."

He pulled back and grinned at her. "I'm guessing you have to be on your best behavior until you accomplish your damned objective. But I warn you, it's a fool's errand. Granny won't sell."

"If you're really so worried about me talking to her, I could take *you* to meet the prospective buyer one day next week. You wouldn't have to tell Isobel right away."

"Oh, no," he said, grimacing. "I don't do secrets. They never end well. If we're doing this, we'll be upfront about your agenda."

"Mr. Chester asked me to present the offer. I'm not responsible for the outcome."

"If you say so." He kept an arm around her waist as they walked out to the car. "Granny is beside herself with excitement that you're coming. I suppose I hadn't realized how much she has missed Brody and Cate and the baby since they left. With just me around, the house has been too quiet."

"Maybe I could have lunch with her one day."

He gave her a sideways frown. "Are you suggesting that idea as a lawyer or as a decent human being?"

"The two aren't mutually exclusive," Abby said, glaring at him.

He helped her into the car and closed her door. Even when she was mad at him, he felt a sexual pull. That reality didn't bode well for his peace of mind.

When he was behind the wheel with the engine running, he apologized. "I'm sorry. No more cheap shots about your profession today, I promise."

She grinned wryly. "Only today?"

He shrugged, feeling lighthearted and pumped about the evening to come. "I'll take the rest of the calendar under consideration, I swear."

The trip up the mountain was quick. When they arrived, Abby stepped out of the car and stared at his grandparents' house in admiration. "I'd forgotten how beautiful it is up here. I've never been inside, though."

"Some of the exterior upkeep has been let go. Brody and I put a lot of sweat equity into cutting back bushes and fixing gutters…things like that. For a long time after Grandda died, Granny couldn't bring herself to stay here with him gone. But now that she's back, she's happy again. This house was something they built together, just like the business."

After unlocking the front door, he stood aside for Abby to enter. He tossed his keys into a carved wooden bowl on a table in the foyer and motioned for Abby to follow him. Raising his voice, he called out. "Granny. We're here."

He'd half expected his grandmother to be hovering by the front door, ready to greet her guest. "She's probably in the kitchen."

"I love all the artwork," Abby said. "Everything is warm and welcoming, but so very unique."

"Aye," Duncan replied, half-distracted. "They collected paintings and sculptures from all over the world. *Granny.* Where are you?" He rounded the corner into the kitchen, and his heart stopped. A small figure lay crumpled in the center of the floor.

"Granny!" He fell to his knees, his heart pounding. "God, Granny. Call 9-1-1," he yelled, though Abby was at his elbow, her eyes wide, her expression aghast.

While Abby fumbled with her cell phone and punched in the numbers, Duncan took his grandmother's hands and chafed them. "Talk to me, Granny. Open your eyes." Abby finished her brief conversation. "Get me a wet cloth," he said. "The drawer by the sink."

Moments later, she crouched at his side and handed him a damp square of cotton. Duncan placed it on his grandmother's forehead. Her lips were blue. His heart slugged in his chest. CPR. He needed to do CPR. He'd had the training. Instinct kicked in. He began the sequence of compressions and breaths. Counting. Pushing. Praying.

Abby took one of Isobel's frails wrists and held it. Duncan shot her a wild-eyed glance. "Anything?"

"No." Tears welled in Abby's eyes but didn't fall.

"Damn it." He repeated the CPR sequence again. And again. Until his chest ached and his arms ached and his heart was broken. "I just talked to her half an hour ago." This couldn't be happening. It wasn't real.

Abby put her arms around him from behind and laid her cheek against his. "I think she's dead, Duncan," she whispered. "I'm sorry. I'm so very sorry."

Five

Abby hadn't realized she could hurt so badly for a man she had known for such a short time. The two hours that followed were nothing less than a nightmare. A parade passed through the house... EMTs and ambulance drivers and Isobel's personal physician and eventually a representative from the local funeral home. At long last, the elderly woman's tiny, cold body was zipped into a dreadful black bag and loaded into the back of a hearse.

If she'd had a choice, Abby wouldn't have chosen to witness that last part, but Duncan wouldn't leave his grandmother and Abby wouldn't leave Duncan. Somewhere along the way, he had withdrawn inside himself. He spoke when necessary. He thanked everyone who helped. He made decisions. He signed papers. But the man who had picked her up at her home earlier that evening was gone.

At last, they were alone. The sprawling house echoed with silence and tragedy.

"You should eat something," Abby said quietly. "Let me fix you a plate."

He didn't respond. She wasn't even sure he heard her.

They had been standing at the front of the house watching as the vehicle bearing his grandmother's body drove away. Quietly, Abby closed and locked the door and took Duncan's arm. "Let's go to the kitchen," she said. "I'll make us some coffee."

As soon as they entered the room, she winced. It was impossible not to remember seeing the small, sad body lying forlorn and alone in the middle of the floor. The doctor believed Isobel likely suffered a massive cardiac event and had died instantly without suffering.

Abby had searched Duncan's face to see if this news brought him comfort. Nothing in his anguished expression told her that was the case.

Now, as Duncan stood irresolute, she eased him toward a chair. "Sit," she said firmly, as she would with a child. She bustled about the unfamiliar kitchen, finding plates and cups and silverware. By the time the coffee brewed, she had scooped out small portions of the appetizers that were to have been Isobel's contribution to the evening's social hour. Baked Brie with raspberry jam. Fresh minced tomato and mozzarella on bruschetta. Mushrooms stuffed with sausage and ricotta.

She put a plate in front of Duncan and laid her

hand on his shoulder. "Try to eat something," she said. He stared at the food, but he didn't see it. That was painfully obvious.

Her heart breaking for him, she poured two cups of steaming coffee, carried them to the table and sat down beside him. She took his hand in both of hers, worried that his long fingers were cold. "Talk to me, Duncan," she said quietly. "Talk to me."

He blinked as if waking from a dream. "She was with me at the office this afternoon. She was fine. I talked to her on the phone after five. She was fine. How could this happen?"

"Miss Izzy was an old woman. I guess her heart gave out."

"I should have been here."

She heard the reproach in his voice. She understood it. But it stung, even so. Duncan was hurting, and he needed a place to direct his pain.

"You heard the doctor. He thinks she died instantly."

Duncan's eyes flashed. "But she shouldn't have died alone."

There was nothing to say to that.

Abby picked up a fork and forced down a few bites of food, though she didn't really feel like eating at all. She was hoping that Duncan would follow her example by rote. After a few moments, he did. He cleared half of what was on his plate, drank one whole cup of coffee and poured himself a second one. Then he paced the kitchen, his agitation increasing by the moment.

Abby was at a loss. "Should we call your brother and your father?" she asked.

He glanced at his watch. "They'll all be asleep by now. No need to wake them. Granny was very specific about her funeral arrangements. The entire family came en masse for Grandda's services. She was honored and glad to have us here. But she insisted that when her time came, no one was to come back to the States. She wanted to be cremated and have her ashes spread on top of the mountain."

Suddenly, Duncan walked out of the kitchen. She followed him. His mood was volatile, so she was worried. Down the hall, he opened the door to his grandmother's bedroom and stood there. Not entering. Only looking. Her bed was neatly made. The novel she had been reading earlier, perhaps before napping, lay facedown on the mattress.

Abby slipped an arm around his waist, trying without words to offer comfort where there was none. A minute passed. Then another.

Duncan was immovable, a statue in a house that had become a mausoleum. When he finally spoke, his words were barely audible. "Do you think she knew how reluctant I was to come here and stay? That I didn't really want to learn the business? That my heart wasn't in it?"

The guilt-ridden questions came from the depths of his grief.

Abby leaned her cheek against his arm and sighed. "Your grandmother adored you, Duncan. The fact that you were willing to give up everything to move here and help her run Stewart Properties made her happier than she had been since your grandfather died. She didn't see your doubts, Duncan. All she saw was a grandson's devotion."

"I hope so."

Abby juggled her own share of guilt. She mourned Isobel's passing for the family's sake. But for Abby, this sudden change meant that Duncan would not be staying in Candlewick. The idea of an affair with the wealthy, charismatic Scotsman had never been realistic from the beginning. Now, though, all the delicious *might-have-beens* were gone for good.

Duncan's posture was rigid. Grief was hard for a man, especially one as masculine and dominant as a Stewart clansman. Abby feared for his mental well-being. The blow of this untimely death so soon after the trauma of uprooting his life and relocating to the States had clearly shaken him to the foundations.

She stroked his arm. He was in shock, whether he realized it or not. His thinking was muddled, his emotions on overload. "Come to the den," she said softly. "Sit and rest. We could watch a movie. Or talk."

Duncan shook his head as if trying to wake up from a dream. "I should take you home," he said, his tone oddly formal. "Let me get my keys."

Abby got in front of him and made him look her in the eyes. "I'm not leaving you alone tonight, Duncan. There are half a dozen bedrooms. I can sleep anywhere. But I won't walk away and let you rattle around this big old house by yourself."

"I'm not a child." His gaze was slightly unfocused, his voice rough, as though normal speech was difficult.

She went up on her tiptoes and kissed his cheek. "I know that. But you're hurting, and no one should have to bear this alone."

In the end, she wasn't much help at all. Though she

managed to get him into the den, he merely stared at the TV screen blankly for hours, unseeing. She might as well have shown him old Bugs Bunny cartoons or sitcom reruns. He would never have known the difference.

At eleven, she powered down the electronics and began turning off lights. She touched his arm. "Why don't you go take a shower, Duncan? It might make you feel better. In the morning, I'll help you with whatever decisions you have to make. Tonight, though, you need sleep."

He nodded and stood, but his compliance seemed illusory at best.

When Duncan was safely in his bedroom, Abby wandered through the house, checking doors and windows. There was an alarm system, but she had no idea how to arm it. Maybe for one night it wouldn't matter.

Finding a guest room was not difficult. Isobel Stewart and her late husband had entertained out-of-town company often. The suite Abby picked at random was decorated beautifully, though a tad formally for her tastes, in deep burgundy and navy. The bathroom had been updated in recent years. All of the necessary amenities were available in drawers and cabinets, including the kind of shower cap hotels offered.

She took a shower, brushed her teeth and put her same clothes back on. Tomorrow, Lara would bring her a small bag of essentials. Earlier, she had sent a brief text to let her friend know what had happened. Lara's rapid, heartfelt response was one small note of sunshine in a horribly gloomy experience.

At last, she folded back the covers on the large,

opulent bed and slipped between the sheets. Sleep should have come easily. Adrenaline and emotional exhaustion had left her feeling wrung out. Even so, she couldn't settle. Her ears strained to hear any sound from Duncan's bedroom. He was almost directly across the hall from her. She had left her door open a crack so she would know if he stirred.

Her premonitions were on target. At 1:00 a.m., she awoke to the sound of someone prowling about in the hallway. In the distance, the kitchen lights came on. Various rustling noises told her Duncan might be getting a snack. He must be hungry. What he had eaten earlier was hardly enough to keep a grown man going for very long.

She debated joining him. Scrambled eggs could be considered comfort food at this hour. She could fix him a light breakfast. But soon, the lights were out again, and she heard him go back to his room.

The disruption of her slumber, coupled with her concern for Duncan, made going *back* to sleep almost impossible. Frustrated, she got up and used the bathroom. Then she stood in the center of the bedroom in the dark and pondered what to do. Was he sleeping? Had he slept at all?

Tomorrow would be another long, difficult day. In this situation, even strong adults sometimes needed help from a doctor in the form of a sleep aid. Not that Duncan would take kindly to that suggestion.

When she heard his door open a second time, she stepped into the hall without second-guessing herself. Duncan jerked backward, startled. "Why are you up?" he growled.

Abby wrapped her arms around her waist and shrugged. "I heard you. I was worried."

"I'm sorry I woke you. You should have gone home."

She wouldn't let his harsh words hurt her. She couldn't. He was lashing out because he didn't know what to do with the emotions tearing at him. "Have you slept at all, Duncan?"

"On and off."

They stood there in the narrow hallway. Duncan wore nothing but a pair of flannel sleep pants that hung low on his hips. His broad chest was bare. His hair stood on end. Though there was not enough light to see for sure, Abby knew his jaw was covered with stubble. The scent of his skin, warm from his bed, wafted in the air between them.

"Duncan, I—"

He held up a hand, cutting her off. "Don't bother. I've said it all to myself, and nothing helps. She was old. Old people die. I get it. But I wasn't ready. And I didn't know it would feel like this." He dropped his head and stared at the floor, dejection and sorrow in every angle of his big, masculine frame.

Abby's heart clenched and ached. He was so very much alone and so very far from home. She took his hand before she could change her mind. "I'm going to lie down with you," she said firmly. "On top of the covers. That way you won't be alone. It helps, I think, to have someone close when you face a loss."

It was a mark of his utter desolation that he didn't protest. Nor did he make some silly male comment about her climbing into bed with him. If anything, the vibe she got from him was gratitude, not that he actually expressed it in so many words.

His bed was a king. The covers were rumpled as if he had fought with them for hours. Together they straightened the sheets and comforter. Without asking, Duncan fetched an extra blanket from the closet. Then he climbed into bed. The light in the bathroom was still on with the door pulled almost completely closed. Abby didn't mention it. Whether an oversight or not, that tiny beam of light was comforting in this dark, dark night.

When Duncan was settled, Abby lay down on top of the covers on the opposite side of the bed and pulled the spare blanket around herself.

Duncan reached out a hand and turned off the lamp. "Thank you, Abby."

The tone in his voice made her want to cry. "You're welcome," she whispered.

The next time she surfaced, it was still dark outside. Confused and disoriented, she blinked and moved restlessly until her memory came crashing back. She was in Duncan's bedroom…in his bed. A noise had awakened her.

She froze for a moment. Was it an intruder? Had her failure to set the alarm left them vulnerable?

For long seconds, she listened. And then it came again. A keening, terrible sound. The sound of a man in the throes of a nightmare.

Duncan flung an arm over his head and cried out. She could *feel* the agony of his dream.

Throwing her blanket aside, she scooted across the mattress and approached him carefully, not wanting to make things worse…certainly not wanting to embarrass him. She put her hand on his arm and spoke his name. "Duncan. Wake up, Duncan. It's me, Abby."

It took several tries, but finally he shuddered and opened his eyes. His face was damp. "Did I dream it?" he asked hoarsely. "Is it true?"

Abby's throat hurt. "I don't know what you dreamed. But if you're asking me about your grandmother, then yes. She's gone."

"Bloody hell." His voice broke on the second word.

Abby couldn't help herself. She scooted beneath the covers and wrapped her arms around him. He buried his face in her neck, shaking. She stroked his hair. "Ssshhh," she said. "It's okay, Duncan. It's going to be okay."

For the first time, she saw him as something other than the wealthy grandson of a wealthy family for whom everything in life had come easily.

He was just a man.

The clock on the bedside table marked the passage of time. Abby drifted in and out of sleep. Duncan slept, as well. She heard his heavy breathing. She felt the weight of his limbs. And with every hour that passed, she knew her own personal grief—grief for the relationship that would wither on the vine before it had a chance to take root.

For whatever reason, Duncan Stewart spoke to something deep in her heart, some vulnerable, fragile, hopeful spot that wanted a man with a voice like warm honey and a deep streak of honor and a strength that would care for a woman and yet respect her ability to care for him, also.

None of it mattered. He wasn't hers to keep.

When her arm went numb, she tried to ease it out from under him. His bare chest radiated heat. Since she was fully dressed, she was too hot. When she tried to push the covers aside, Duncan muttered and rolled toward her, one powerful leg trapping both of hers against the mattress.

In a single stark second, she felt the press of his aroused sex against her hip. *Oh, Lordy.* Her stomach flip-flopped. Duncan was asleep. She knew that. A man's body had certain predictable reactions in compromising situations.

Was this *her* fault? Had she subconsciously wanted this?

No. Heck, no. She might be a sex-starved single woman with few prospects, but she wasn't that desperate. She had wanted to help Duncan through the night. That was all. Besides, she was fully dressed. Nothing could happen.

He mumbled something unintelligible and slid a hand underneath her sweater.

Abby froze, her breath catching in her throat. When Duncan cupped her breast and stroked her nipple through her thin, satiny bra, her brain shut down. It felt so damned good she wanted to groan out loud. But that might wake him up, and how would she explain the current situation?

Duncan murmured a word, a Gaelic word. It sounded like sunshine and warm breezes and a man's intent. Abby melted inside, her good intentions winnowing away like sand castles at high tide.

She tried, she really did. "Duncan," she whispered. "I don't think you want to do this." She cupped his face in her hands, feeling the rough growth of a day's beard. Her lips brushed his cheek, the bridge of his nose. "Wake up, Duncan. Please."

"I'm awake," he muttered. Now he pushed the bra to her armpits and found her bare breasts. He palmed one. Then the other. "Gorgeous," he said. "So beautiful."

Abby forgot to breathe. Her entire body went liquid with pleasure. His fingers teased the tips of her breasts. Tugging, twisting. Then he bent and tasted her, scraping his teeth against her sensitive flesh and biting gently.

When she cried out, he ripped at her sweater, dragging it and her bra over her head in short order, tangling her hair and leaving her naked from the waist up. Now her remaining clothing frustrated him.

Abby knew they were careening down a dangerous slope. "Duncan, please."

He froze, his chest heaving. He reared up on one elbow. His free hand was at her waistband, struggling with the fastening on her pants.

His eyes were open. In the faint illumination from the bathroom light, they glittered with intent. "Are ye asking me to stop, lass?"

It was up to her. She could stand up and walk away, and nothing would happen. The hushed silence after his question seemed to last forever, though it was probably only seconds that passed.

She was defeated by his misery and his raw need and her own yearning. Everything inside her wanted to give him peace and release. She wanted that and more for herself. She wasn't going to have Duncan

Stewart for any kind of happily-ever-after. But she could have tonight. She *would* have it.

"No." She swallowed hard, trying to find her breath, her courage. "Don't stop."

Six

Under the circumstances, she expected Duncan to rush madly toward the finish line. He was sleep-deprived and grief stricken and a man at the end of his emotional and physical reserves.

Duncan had other ideas.

As she lay trembling and aghast that she hadn't been smart enough to stop this madness, he unbuttoned and unzipped her pants, dragged them down her legs and tossed them aside. Now she wore nothing but a pair of fairly ordinary bikini panties.

Duncan pressed two fingertips to the damp fabric covering her sex. She was glad it was dark. Suddenly, she was conscious of her convex tummy and her rounded thighs. He stroked her through the fabric, making her squirm. "I've no' ever seen a more beautifully feminine woman, Abby Hartmann. Ye're like a feast for my hands and my eyes. I want to gobble you up, and I don't know where to start."

"You could just get on with it," she muttered. She hadn't expected him to linger over the first course.

He stood up long enough to remove his pajama pants but came back to her immediately, dragging her into his embrace and burying his face in her hair. "I wanted you the first moment I saw you, Abby." He kissed the shell of her ear, his breath hot on her neck. "I don't think you have a clue what you do to a man. You're soft and warm and curvy, all the things I'm not. Women are special creatures, beautiful and rare."

If any American man of her acquaintance had uttered those words, she might have laughed. Duncan's sleep-roughened voice and rolling accent made everything he said plausible.

Then he lapsed into Gaelic and Abby lost her head completely. "Duncan…" she whispered his name, arching her back as he kissed his way from her nose to her chin to her throat and then paused to enjoy her cleavage.

For a hazy moment, she wondered if she were dreaming. The line between fact and fiction had been blurred tonight. She slid her hands into his hair, winnowing her fingers through the thick, healthy strands…feeling the strong bones of his skull.

His naked body touched hers everywhere, it seemed. She felt the damp warmth of his skin, tasted the salt of his sweat, heard the harshness of his breathing as his arousal mounted and her own raced to meet and match it. Despite her self-consciousness, for one wild instant, she wanted to turn on every light in the room and feast her eyes on the work of art that was Duncan Stewart.

He smelled like a man in the best possible way, and in his utter dominance, her femininity unfurled, reveling in the absolute freedom to take what she wanted and demand what she needed.

When her fingernails raked his back, Duncan choked out a laugh. "Have a care, little cat. You'll leave a scar. Is that what you want?"

It was a joke, a lighthearted sexual tease. Her own response stunned her. If marking a man was a primal instinct, then yes. The thought of any other woman having Duncan made her heart weep.

She soothed the scratches with gentle touches. "My apologies, Mr. Stewart. It's your own fault. You make me a little crazy."

"Only a little? I'll have to try harder." He kissed her unexpectedly, his tongue stroking deeply into the recesses of her mouth and stealing every bit of oxygen from her lungs. It was a kiss that lasted forever and yet ended far too soon—in turns sweet and coaxing, then forceful and demanding.

He moved on top of her now, spreading her legs with his hips, but not joining their bodies. Abby felt faint, half-asleep, wholly dizzy with drugged arousal. She wound her arms around his neck, clinging to the only anchor in the room. Everything else spun dizzily.

Duncan reached between their bodies and fingered her gently. She was so slick and ready it was almost embarrassing. With an exclamation that might have been a Gaelic curse, he centered the head of his erection at her entrance and pushed steadily.

* * *

Duncan had never been very good at self-deception. He knew what he was doing, and he knew there would be repercussions. But he couldn't have walked away from Abby even to save his own life. In that moment, she was everything to him.

Her body gloved him in warm, clenching heat. His life was a shit-storm of pain and regret at the moment. Abby offered absolution and escape. He chose the latter without shame or regret. He had wanted her before today. Now he needed her, as well.

"Am I hurting you?" he groaned. She was tight and so small in his big bed. His height topped hers by at least a dozen inches.

Abby shook her head. "No." She toyed with the hair at his nape, sending lightning bolts of heat down his spine to join the conflagration elsewhere.

"God, you're sweet," he groaned. "I could keep you in this bed for days." Reality tried to intrude. He ruthlessly pushed it away.

She canted her hips, forcing him deeper. "I won't break," she said, the words shaky. "You don't have to be so careful with me."

"I don't want to hurt you," he said roughly, still moving in her as if he could take her like this again and again until dawn. For hours, he had slammed every door that kept his emotions in check. Now Abby's very softness and transparent caring made his self-protective instincts for naught. He knew she was here to comfort him. He knew, and he took her anyway. What kind of man did that make him?

Abby sensed his distress and cradled his face in her hands. "Don't think, Duncan. Only feel. You and me. In this bed. Maybe we're dreaming, right? Maybe this is as good as it gets. Show me everything, you big stubborn Scotsman. Make me fly."

He lost his head after that. His body took over, recklessly chasing a wicked, shocking release that was destined to destroy him so completely he would never be himself again. He felt the press of her bosom against his chest. He smelled the faint scent of her hair and her perfume.

Her body cradled his perfectly, welcoming his wild lust and transmuting it into something far more un-expected and dangerous. He plunged into her again and again, thrusting himself against the head of her womb until she cried out and shuddered in his arms.

He waited for her orgasm to take its course. Then he released the almost-superhuman hold he had kept on his own body and groaned her name as he emp-tied himself into her keeping.

When he woke up, sunlight filled the room, and Abby was gone. Duncan's head throbbed, though he had consumed no alcohol. Memories swam in his brain with disturbing, drunken chaos. His grandmoth-er's still, cold shape on the floor. The doctor's sym-pathetic gaze. Abby's warm, naked body in his bed.

God, what had he done?

To give himself time to steady his careening emo-tions, he took a shower, shaved and then sat down in a chair beside the bed with his cell phone. Staring at it, he prepared a speech for his brother and his father. This was tough news to deliver over the phone, par-ticularly from such a distance.

It hurt to think about Abby right now. His relationship with her, such as it was, represented every bit of guilt he felt about his grandmother. Had he made a huge mistake? Was Abby the enemy in this situation? Did she have a secret agenda? Or were her compassion and gentle caring sincere?

Because he didn't know the answer to any of those questions, he shoved them aside and dialed his brother's number. Today was going to be long and difficult. He might as well get started.

Abby left Duncan's bed just before dawn, slipping from his embrace with every care not to wake him. She needn't have worried. He slept deeply, sprawled on his back, his body completely relaxed.

It wouldn't last. She knew that. But at least she had given him a few hours of peace and oblivion. Perhaps that would sustain him through the ordeal to follow.

She went back to her own room and dozed until eight thirty. Then she freshened up and made a plan with Lara via text. When that was done, she scrounged in the kitchen for something to eat. Duncan's bedroom door was closed. She would not intrude.

After eating a banana and a cup of yogurt that she didn't really taste, she went back to her bedroom and called in to work, requesting a few days of vacation. It was a bad time with Mr. Chester out, but he would understand. Isobel Stewart had been a client for decades. Her family certainly deserved an extra measure of attention and care under the circumstances.

At ten, Duncan still had not appeared. It seemed foolish to worry about a grown man. But Abby began to second-guess herself. Was he hoping she would go away so they wouldn't have to face each other?

When Lara arrived, Abby hurried to the front of the house to meet her friend outside. She didn't want to disturb Duncan's privacy.

The morning was crisp and cool. At these altitudes, the first frost would soon dust the rhododendron thickets with white. Lara jumped out of the car and hugged her friend tightly. "Are you okay, honey? This must have been a terrible shock."

Abby hadn't realized she was so close to the edge. Lara's concern broke down her defenses, and she burst into tears, tears born of stress and lack of sleep and uncertainty about the days to come.

Lara let her cry, patting her back and holding her close. At last, Abby pulled away and wiped her nose. "I'm sorry. I didn't know that was going to happen."

"You look like hell, darlin'. No offense."

"None taken." Abby shook her head. "I've never seen a dead person before, Lara…at least not one that hasn't been all prettied up in a casket. It was awful. Poor Miss Izzy. Duncan is drowning in guilt that she died alone, and I can't say that I blame him. I feel pretty awful about it, too. She was excited about me coming by to see her. I've worried that it was too much."

Lara took her by the shoulders and gave her a little shake. "Don't be a goose. Most elderly people I know would think this kind of death was a great blessing. No lingering illness. No nursing home. No loss of independence. Miss Izzy died happy. Her grandson moved here to run the company with her. She had everything to live for. I guess her heart gave out. And now she's with Mr. Stewart, the love of her life."

"I hope Duncan will find comfort in that thought.

He's very upset. It was so sudden. She was at work with him yesterday. They had talked on the phone right before he picked me up. Then we got here, and she was on the floor..." Abby put her fist to her mouth, reliving those awful moments.

Lara curled an arm around her again. "There are worse things in life than death. Duncan will make peace with this. But it will take some time, perhaps."

"I want to help him," Abby said. "With all he has to do. Is that weird?"

Lara pursed her lips. "Well, I don't know. Is he going to let you?"

It was a good question. And one Abby couldn't answer. She pointed to the back seat. "Is that my suitcase?"

Lara nodded and lifted it out. "I packed in a hurry, but I think you've got enough for a couple of days. Plus, it's not like you don't live close. If you think you'll need your car, let me know, and I'll figure out a way to get it up here to you."

Abby shook her head in bemusement. "You have the best heart of anyone I know, Lara. I don't know why you have to pretend all the time that you're a hard-ass."

The other woman held up a hand, her expression alarmed. "You keep those wretched opinions to yourself, you hear?"

"Understood." Abby hesitated, feeling her neck heat. "There's one more thing."

Lara nodded. "Anything for you, cupcake. Name it."

"My father came by the house the other evening. I've changed the locks on all the doors. And I didn't let him in. Will you please drive by occasionally and see if everything looks okay?"

"Damn it, Abby. Get a restraining order."

"That would be public and embarrassing."

"You went to court and legally changed your last name to your mother's maiden name to distance yourself from him. What's the big deal about one more step? One more piece of paper? You shouldn't have to live in fear."

"He's not dangerous. I don't think."

Lara scowled. "He's dangerous to your peace of mind. That's enough for me to want him gone for good. So, yes. I'll check on the house. Anything else?"

Abby's eyes welled with tears, her emotions too near the surface. "Thank you, Lara. You're the best."

"Well, of course I am."

The other woman leaned into the front of the car and extracted a large picnic basket. "Mama and I got up early and started cooking. I know it's just Duncan, and you of course, so we didn't go overboard. But there's fried chicken and green beans and corn. Plus, rolls and baked apples and pecan pie. Should be enough there for two or three meals if you don't want to leave the house. Call me if there's anything in particular he needs. Folks in town want to help, but they don't know him very well. I promised I'd stay in touch with you."

Abby nodded. Small communities like Candlewick were known for their generous support in times of crisis. The Stewart heir would receive many kindnesses, even if he didn't expect anything to come his way.

She rested the suitcase on the wooden settee on the porch and picked up the picnic basket. "I should go inside and check on Duncan. I haven't seen him yet this morning."

"He was probably up most of the night after a shock like that. I'm sure I would have been if it were me."

Abby bit her lip and swallowed the need to blurt out the truth. Some stories were far too personal to share, even with a beloved girlfriend. "Thanks for everything, Lara. I'll call you later today when I know something."

She waved as her friend drove away, and then turned to set the suitcase just inside the front door. After that she picked up the heavy woven basket, closed the door with her hip and carried the food to the kitchen. Lara's mom had written out careful instructions for how to refrigerate and reheat each item.

When Abby rounded the corner and entered the room, Duncan was standing there, staring at the floor. He seemed calm, but she couldn't read his expression. She cleared her throat. "My friend Lara brought lunch," she said. "I just need to put a few things away."

His head jerked up, and he flushed. He pulled the basket out of her grip and set it aside. Then he took her by the waist and set her up on the counter. His gaze was clear and direct and troubled. "I'm sorry, Abby. About last night. It never should have happened. I've been trying to figure out how to apologize."

There was no warning, no preparation for this confrontation. Her heart shredded and her stomach shrank. He was too close. She felt raw. Exposed. "No apology needed," she croaked. "It was a difficult few hours."

He brushed the back of his hand over her cheek. "You saved my life last night, and you don't even know it. But I let it go too far."

"There were two of us in that bed," she snapped. "Don't play the noble hero. It was no big deal."

His eyes narrowed. "You're angry."

Maybe so, but not for the reasons he thought. She scrambled for composure. These next few days would depend on her ability to keep things light. "Neither of us meant for anything to happen last night, Duncan. Let's call it extenuating circumstances. You didn't take advantage of me. I don't want your apologies. Still, my firm will be handling your grandmother's probate, so it's probably a good idea for us to establish some boundaries."

"I agree." His tone was formal, his gaze frosty. "On another note, we didn't use protection. You should know that I'm in good health."

Abby's face flamed. Never in a million years had she imagined herself in the midst of such a conversation. "As am I," she said. "It was an unfortunate lapse, but I'm on the Pill for other reasons, so pregnancy isn't a worry."

"That's good."

"Yes."

Despite the negative tenor of their conversation, he still stood in the vee of her outspread knees. Though he wasn't touching her, they breathed the same oxygen. He ran a hand through his hair, betraying possible frustration. "I've spoken to my family."

"How did that go?"

"They were shocked, of course. And sad. No one is ever prepared for the fact that goodbyes are sometimes not an option."

"What happens next?" She hopped down from the counter, forcing him to step back. Without waiting for permission, she began putting away the food Lara had brought.

"I have a problem," Duncan said. "I don't know what to do."

She closed the refrigerator door and stared at him. "What's wrong?"

"I told you Granny wanted to be cremated."

"Yes."

"But it doesn't make sense. Grandda is buried in the cemetery in town. There's a plot beside him. People want to pay their respects at a funeral, both former and current employees. Some of them worked for my grandparents for decades. Why wouldn't I have a traditional funeral so her friends could say goodbye?"

"Do you have any idea why she mentioned cremation? Was there some significance to having her ashes scattered on top of the mountain?"

"I don't think so. If I had to guess, I'd say she wanted to make things easier for our family. No funeral, no problem. Or maybe she was simply trying to be economical."

"Old people get that way sometimes, even when they have nothing to worry about financially."

"Yes. They do."

"Well, at the risk of seeming disrespectful, I'd say what matters is the choice that feels right to *you*. She's gone. You're here. If you think a traditional funeral is the way to go, then do it."

He nodded slowly. "I will." His expression lightened. "Thanks, Abby. I hadn't expected all these decisions. It's a lot. I don't want to make a mistake. I want to honor her memory…hers *and* Grandda's." Before she could stop him, he reached out and pulled her into a bear hug. "Thank you for being here with me."

Seven

Duncan used his gratitude shamelessly as an excuse to touch her again. Abby was right. They couldn't carry on an affair under the circumstances. But God, he wanted to feel her in his arms again.

He stroked her hair, but other than that, behaved himself.

Last night had taken him to the depths and then at the last moment, thrown him a life raft in the form of sexy, curvaceous, kindhearted Abby Hartmann. Even now, the memories made him hard. He released her reluctantly. "I have to go to the funeral home at one o'clock to view the body. I picked out a casket online this morning, and the dress shop in town sent over a fall suit that Granny would have liked. I wanted her to have something new. But there are a few other things that require my attention. Come with me. Please."

"Of course." She wrapped her arms around her waist, visibly uncomfortable. "I've taken a week off from work, Duncan. I want to help you any way I can."

"But not sleep with me."

"Of course not!"

He smiled wryly. "Just making sure." Tormenting Abby was one of the few pleasures he had left. Besides, he still wasn't sure if she was an angel come to save him or a cagey lawyer with her own reasons for hanging around. He wanted to believe she was innocent and pure, but he could swear she was keeping secrets from him, and that raised all sorts of red flags. "I'm starving," he said. "Let's see what your friend brought us."

Over a home-cooked meal that was better than anything he had tasted in his entire life, Abby grilled him.

"What will you do with the house?" she asked.

He took a sip of water and grabbed another chicken leg. "I don't know. But whether I sell it tomorrow or a year from now, it has to be cleaned out. My grandparents weren't hoarders, but they were married for a long, long time. There are closets and cabinets and drawers..." He shook his head, shuddering. "Brody and Cate helped Granny get started with some of it, but they barely scratched the surface. It's going to be a mess."

"Do you feel like you have to deal with it personally? For sentimental reasons?"

"Oh, no. Not at all. A few months ago, Granny gave Brody and me some mementos of our grandfather. Beyond that, we're guys. We don't care about dishes and such. I think the best thing is to take all the clothing and linens to charity and then have a big estate sale."

"I could help with emptying the drawers and closets and bagging up the things to give away."

"And I'll have to do Grandda's office myself."

"Is a week enough time?"

"I think it will have to be."

Abby didn't press about the business, and he was glad. By every standard, he should be relieved that he could sell and walk away. But somehow, now that his grandmother was gone so suddenly, it didn't seem that easy.

When the meal was done, they cleaned up the kitchen in silence and put the food away. He touched her arm. "The funeral is going to be tomorrow afternoon at two. I didn't see any reason to wait. Sunday afternoon is a time most people are free."

"Makes sense."

He played with a strand of her hair, unable to keep away from her despite his best judgment. "When it's done, let's go to Asheville overnight. To that big, fancy hotel I've heard about. We'll have a nice dinner, relax and come home on Monday to tackle all this."

She looked up at him, her eyes huge. "You're asking me to go away to a hotel with you?"

"We could reserve two rooms." But he didn't want to...

"I'm getting very mixed signals from you, Duncan."

He grimaced. "I know."

"Funerals are grueling. You'll need a break afterward."

"Is that a yes?"

Her gaze searched his face as if looking for answers he couldn't give her. The whole situation was screwed up. It made no sense at all to get further involved with Abby. The only reason he had come to Candlewick in the first place was for his grandmother. Now, that reason was gone. Complicating matters further was the reality that Abby's legal firm would push the idea of selling the business immediately. Duncan needed time to process what he had lost.

Abby sighed, leaning into his chest for a brief moment before stepping away self-consciously and puttering at the sink. "Lara brought me a suitcase of clothes and other necessities. I think I'll shower and change. I'll be ready whenever you want to leave."

She escaped, leaving Duncan to realize that she had never actually said yes to the Asheville idea.

Viewing his grandmother's body turned out to be much more heart-wrenching than he had expected. She seemed even smaller in death. Abby stayed at his shoulder the entire time—at one point, slipping her hand into his.

He squeezed it. "She was a formidable lady. She and Grandda let Brody and me stay with them for several months when our parents divorced. She gave us sympathy and support, but she didn't coddle us. That was the Scots in her. She knew we had to be tough in a tough world."

He turned suddenly and looked down at Abby. "I'm sorry. This must bring back memories of losing your mother."

She shook her head. "No. I was too young. But

I *will* admit to having a distaste for funeral homes. Something about the smells and the creaky floors and the guys in suits. Maybe we should do the whole Norse funeral-pyre thing and put our loved ones on flaming boats and send them out to sea."

"You do realize that Candlewick is in the mountains."

"It's a metaphor," she said, resting her head on his shoulder for a brief moment. "Work with me, Duncan."

He bent and kissed his grandmother's cheek. "I love you, Granny. Godspeed. Give Grandda a big hug from Brody and me."

The funeral home employee stood several feet away, discreetly waiting for his cue to close the casket.

Duncan hesitated. Watching that lid go down was not something he wanted to witness. He gave the man an apologetic glance. "We'll step outside if you don't mind."

In the hallway, he felt oddly dizzy. He hadn't signed on for this. Running Stewart Properties was one thing. What did he know about giving his grandmother a proper send-off? What if he did something wrong?

Abby dragged him to a nearby chair. "Sit." She handed him a bottle of water. "It's going to be okay, Duncan."

"Aye." He took a long swig, draining half the container. "I suppose it is. But when?"

Afterward, there was more to be done. All of the paperwork had to be finalized, the flowers ordered, a brief obituary written for the online listing, the Presbyterian minister nailed down for the words of committal and the burial scheduled for immediately after the brief service.

When they finally walked out of the funeral home into the bright autumn sunshine, Duncan felt as if he had gone three rounds with the old bully from his school back home. That huge, blustering kid was the one who taught Duncan to be light on his feet and how to take a blow to the face and keep going.

Looking back, those days were sweet and simple compared to this.

He barely remembered driving up the mountain.

Now, each time he had to return to his grandmother's house was going to be painful. The echoing silence. The memories.

Abby dropped her purse on a chair in the foyer and eyed him with an assessing gaze. "What do you want to do? Get to work? Take a nap? Channel surf in front of the TV?"

He rolled his shoulders. What he really wanted to do was take Abby to bed. His hands trembled with the need to touch her and feel her warm curves against him. "If you're up for it, we could climb the mountain. I haven't been up to the top since Grandda died."

"I love that idea. I went there once with a date a million years ago. We were both in high school. He wanted to impress me. We climbed a fence and ended up in poison ivy. You can imagine the rest."

Duncan laughed, as she had meant him to... "Hopefully, today will be more uneventful."

They changed clothes, grabbed a couple of water bottles and set out. The sun hung low in the sky, but they had plenty of time to get back to the house before dark. Years ago, Geoffrey and Isobel had built a trail all the way to the top of the mountain. They owned several hundred acres of pristine forest. When Duncan sold everything, what would happen to this peaceful wilderness?

The thought troubled him, though it wasn't really his problem.

Abby was in great physical shape, but he had to adjust his stride to accommodate her vertically challenged legs. She wore khaki shorts, a white cotton shirt tied at her waist and tiny leather hiking boots that made her look like a very sexy mountain climber.

He tried not to fixate on her legs. Or on the peeks of her stomach where her shorts and her top separated. The day was hot. She started out with only two buttons undone on her shirt. By the time they made it to the summit, a third one was loose. He liked his odds. Especially when tiny droplets of sweat rolled down between her breasts. He could almost imagine tasting each one.

They found the old weathered bench that had been there forever and flopped down, breathing hard. In front of them, a swath of treetops had been cut out, framing a postcard vista of the town of Candlewick far below.

Abby drained half of her water and wiped her mouth. "I'd forgotten how stunning the view is up here."

The view was definitely stunning, but it was closer to home. The woman beside him far outshone the scenery. Duncan found himself hot and horny and desperately conflicted. He was going back to Scotland very soon. Before—when he'd known he was here in North Carolina for at least two years—he had entertained the possibility of a relationship with the smart, sexy lawyer. The attraction was definitely mutual, and Abby was unattached.

But how fair was it for him to use her sympathy and her generous heart and her gorgeous body to help him through a bad time and then walk away?

When Abby stood to shoot a few photographs with her smartphone, Duncan stayed where he was and brooded. If Abby's boss had his way, Duncan would exit this experience a very wealthy man. He could take a share of his money back to Scotland and invest in Brody's company, perhaps become a full partner. Is that what he wanted?

Abby turned back to him and smiled. "Say cheese." He frowned, but she took the shot anyway. "Something to remember you by," she said lightly.

Had she said it on purpose? To let him know that she knew? They might have blistering chemistry, but their timing sucked. Not to mention the possibly/ probably unethical fact that Abby's boss was going to oversee the disbursement of Isobel Stewart's estate.

When she sat down again at his side, he flinched and put another few inches between them. His mood was volatile. Her nearness was a provocation he couldn't handle in his current mental state.

Abby sighed. "This isn't going to work, is it?"

"I don't know what you mean," he lied with a straight face.

She leapt to her feet and paced. "You're all alone, Duncan. You have a gargantuan task ahead of you, even if you only consider the house and not the business. Your brother has a brand-new wife and an even newer baby. He's in no position to help you with this. From what you've told me of your father, he's far too self-absorbed to drop everything and support his younger son or deal with actual *work*."

He cocked his head. "What are you trying to say, Abby?"

With her hands on her hips, she faced him, cheeks flushed, rose-gold curls tumbling in the breeze. "I'm the only friend you have at the moment. You need me. And I want to help you. But we have this *thing* between us. It's awkward."

"You told me pretty clearly to keep my hands to myself."

"I may have been wrong about that," she said, her expression hard to read. "Or at least unrealistic. Before your grandmother died——when you and I were flirting with the idea of a temporary fling—you were going to be a resident. I was worried about my career. About gossip. But you're leaving Candlewick now...or at least you will be soon. As long as we're discrete, I can't see that anything we do or don't do is anyone's business but ours."

Again, he got the impression she wasn't telling him the whole truth. What was she hiding? What was her endgame?

"I've never been a man who *uses* a woman for sex."

"What do you call it if the woman is using you in return?"

His head snapped back in shock. "Excuse me?"

Abby gazed at him with a wry, self-mocking smile. "I'm not writing a fairy tale here, Duncan. I live in a small town with an extremely limited dating pool. It might be nice for me to enjoy a liaison without worrying about repercussions when it's over. You're like a yummy homemade dessert from a local bakery… with a definite expiration date stamped on the box. You'll be going back to Scotland sooner rather than later. In the meantime, we could fool around."

He gaped at her. "You're propositioning me?"

"I'm sorry if that offends your alpha male sensibilities."

To be honest, it kind of did. He had wanted to pursue her…to convince her. "I'll have to think about it," he said, sounding stiff and pedantic even to his own ears.

"Fine," Abby said. "You do that." Her eyes flashed fire, and her face turned beet red. "I'm going back to the house."

She set off down the trail at a breakneck pace. He was so shocked by her offer and his own stupid response that it took him several minutes to jump up and follow her.

The woman was fast. He'd give her that. They were almost back at the house before he caught up with her, and that was only because a branch had gotten tangled in her hair. She was cursing and pulling and—if he wasn't mistaken—about to cry.

"Steady, lass," he said, sliding his arms around her from behind and stilling her flailing arms. "You're making it worse."

She froze. He held the branch steady with one hand and used the other to separate her hair from its prison, one strand at a time. Then he cupped her face in his hands. "I'm sorry, sweet Abby. You took me by surprise."

She couldn't quite meet his eyes. "It's no big deal. I misread the situation. I'm going home now. You can let me know when and if you need assistance loading boxes and filling garbage bags."

He kissed her forehead. "Don't be mad."

"You don't want me," she said quietly. "I'm not mad. I'm embarrassed."

"Quit being a bloody fool," he shouted. "Of course I want you." A tension headache wrapped his skull in a painful vise.

She looked up at him, blinking, her expression stormy and wounded. "It didn't sound like it. I tend to forget that men don't like pushy women. I'm accustomed to problem solving. I guess I overstepped my bounds. I apologize."

He released her, took a step backward and jammed his hands in his pockets to keep from shaking her. "For the life of me," he growled, "I dinna ken how a woman can be a selfless angel one minute and a contrary mule the next."

Clearly, she didn't like *that* remark. "Go to hell, Duncan. I changed my mind. I wouldn't sleep with you if every last man in Candlewick vanished tomorrow."

She took a step in his direction and thumped a finger into his chest. "You're arrogant and entitled and you think men rule the world. Well, I have news for you, *Mr.* Stewart. That may work in Scotland, but here in America we're—"

He snatched her up and kissed her ruthlessly, not giving any quarter until the fight left her, and she groaned low in her throat and every hair on the back of his neck stood at attention.

Now that he had regained control of the situation—
for the moment—he decided to enjoy his advantage.
Keeping one arm around her, he used his free hand
to unbutton her shirt. "I love your bosom, lass. Have
I told you so?"

"You might have mentioned it," she mumbled.
"And FYI, nobody here calls it that."

He was debating the logistics of baring her lovely
body when he realized her bra had a front closure.
"Sweet heaven," he muttered. With one quick flick
of his wrist, her heavy, pink-tipped breasts spilled
into view. He released her so he could fill his palms
with the pleasing weight of them. "Don't tell me I
don't want you. It's the daftest thing you've ever said
to me."

"I know this is wrong," Abby whispered, her expression equal parts troubled and yearning. "Wrong
time. Wrong place. Wrong man. Wrong woman. But
I don't care."

He scooped her into his arms and strode toward the
house. "I care," he said, breathing heavily, not from
his burden, but from the urgent need to put an end
to this dance. "No more discussion," he said firmly.
"We're on the same page. And if we want to keep it
a secret between us, that's our right. Small towns are
the same the world over. Gossip is the breath of life. I
won't have you tormented when I'm gone."

"I agree," Abby said. "Need-to-know only."

"Put your hand in my pocket. Get the key."

When Abby giggled, his neck heated. "That was a
serious request, lass. I find I don't want to put you down.
I'm afraid you'll run away when I'm not looking."

Abby located the key quickly, and soon he had her

inside with the door closed and locked behind them. "Now what?" she asked, her smoke-gray eyes darker today...filled with secrets.

"I have a really large, fancy shower in my bathroom. Why don't we see if we'll both fit?"

Eight

Abby couldn't decide which was worse: breaking half a dozen ethical codes of conduct or taking advantage of a man who was at a low point in his life. The more frightening thing was…she didn't really care. Some hitherto dormant part of her personality had wrested control from her careful, always-cautious self and decided that this was the year Abby Hartmann was going to have a wild and glorious affair.

Duncan hadn't been kidding about his bathroom. It was a decadent homage to marble and glass. And mirrors. Way too many mirrors. She sucked in her tummy and concentrated on the important things. Like watching her Scots lover undress. He stripped off his clothes with an economy of movement that was elegant and yet deeply masculine. No self-consciousness there.

She already knew that his chest and arms were

golden brown from his days spent on the water. Clearly, not all of his responsibilities involved a boring desk job. Though he was as fair-skinned as she was, he had a light, seemingly permanent tan except for a strip of white around his hips and upper thighs. The dusting of hair on his muscled body had been gilded by the sun.

His erection reared against his belly, long and thick and hard.

Some unknown force sucked all the oxygen out of the bathroom. Spots danced in front of her eyes, and her limbs froze.

Duncan's smile was gentle but knowing. "Don't get shy on me now, Abby. I liked the warrior woman up on the mountain."

Locking gazes with him was too intimate…like staring straight into the sun. She propped her foot on a stool and bent to unlace her boot. "I'm not shy," she muttered. Out of the corner of her eye, she watched him, but he didn't move. When she had removed her sock and shoe, she swapped feet and repeated the process.

Because Duncan had unbuttoned her shirt and unfastened her bra, her breasts bounced when she bent over. It seemed stupid to hide them away again when she was about to get in the shower.

With her feet now bare, she straightened slowly.

Duncan's gaze narrowed. Slashes of red colored his cheekbones. "Take off your clothes," he said. "I want to watch."

A deeply flawed part of her personality refused to let her resist a dare. Duncan's sexual demands challenged her to match his confidence. She lifted one shoulder and let it fall. "No one's stopping you."

She slipped off her shirt and bra and tossed them aside. Shoulders back, chin up, she let him look his fill. When the muscles in his throat worked and his Adam's apple bobbed up and down, she surmised that he was not quite as relaxed as he appeared.

"Now the rest," he said hoarsely.

The shorts had a zipper, one that could be lowered very slowly while a man watched. When the zipper opened as far as it would go, she shimmied the khaki shorts down her hips all the way to her ankles, stepped free, and kicked them aside.

Every wild, rushing impulse in her brain screamed at her to cover herself with her hands. She had never felt more naked or more vulnerable. But then again, she had never been as aroused.

Duncan nodded slowly. He turned and started the water flowing in the shower, adjusting the temperature and testing it with his hand. He faced her again. "Can your hair get wet?"

"I was hoping you might wash it for me."

His erection jerked and bobbed visibly as if her words had been an actual, physical touch. "I could do that. Come here, Abby."

It wasn't far. Five steps. Six at the most. The journey took forever, because her world had skidded into slow motion.

He put his hands at her hips and slid her underwear down her legs. When he knelt at her feet and tapped her ankle, she stepped out of the panties automatically, afraid of what he might do next and equally afraid that he might not.

But nothing happened. Duncan straightened. He pulled her into the shower enclosure, joined her and closed the glass door. The water was warm, but not hot enough to produce an obscuring cloud of steam. Good move on his part. They were drenched in moments.

He reached for a travel-sized bottle of shampoo and squirted it into his hands. "Turn around," he said gruffly.

Given long enough, Abby might have melted like hot wax and slipped down the drain. Having Duncan massage her scalp and neck was one of the most erotic, pleasurable experiences of her life. She felt him behind her, large and tall. Her head fell back against his chest. "Forget sex," she mumbled. "This is amazing."

Chuckling, he turned her to face him and aimed the showerhead to rinse her hair. "I hope you're joking." He took the washcloth and dried her face. "You look about sixteen right now. I didn't realize you had freckles. Just a few." He touched the bridge of her nose. "They're tiny. And cute. Like you."

"I was a mess when I was sixteen. Acne. Braces. Zero confidence. Trust me. It wasn't my best moment."

The water sluiced over his broad shoulders. She wanted to touch him, but despite her bold request on the mountaintop, she found—in this intimate situation—she was regrettably out of her depth.

Duncan's eyes, always dark brown, glittered with hunger. "Touch me, lass. Please."

How could she refuse? How could she let her bold show of feminine courage amount to nothing but words?

Without speaking, she reached for the bar of soap and the second washcloth. When the cotton was wet enough for her liking, she lathered the soap, set the bar aside and took Duncan's hard erection in her palm, wrapping it in the slightly rough fabric of the washcloth.

His breath hissed out in a gasp. At his hips, his hands fisted. His eyes squeezed shut. Carefully, gently, she washed him. First his sex. Then his chest and his neck, and at last his back.

Duncan's entire body was rigid. Neither of them had done a complete head-to-toe. But they had both been under the water long enough to take care of the immediate sweat and dirt from their hike.

When she released him, he stayed where he was, eyes still closed. Clumsily, Abby did a quick swipe of other, more personal areas of her own body. She had spent one night in Duncan's bed, but she didn't feel comfortable enough with him yet to let him wash her in a way that might lead to more than she had bargained for.

Before he could stop her, she opened the glass door. "I'm all clean now. I think I'll dry my hair while you finish up."

As an extra measure of safety, she didn't even remain in Duncan's bathroom. She darted across the hall to her own and began the arduous process of taming her naturally curly hair.

She'd half expected Duncan to follow her after a moment or two. When he didn't, she was disappointed. She finished drying her hair and smoothed the bouncy waves behind her ears.

Grabbing her silky, thigh-length robe out of her

suitcase, she slipped her arms into the sleeves and tied the sash. At the last minute, she scooted back to the bathroom and added a spritz of her favorite perfume.

Then she hovered in the middle of the bedroom and lost her nerve. Biting the edge of her fingernail, she thought of all the reasons she shouldn't have sex with Duncan Stewart. Without him at her side, it was far easier to be sensible. But then again, she was tired of being sensible.

She crossed the carpet, reached for the doorknob and screeched when the door swung inward, the bottom edge catching her bare toes. "Ouch. That hurt."

Duncan, wearing nothing but a strategically placed damp towel, had entered just as she was prepared to go in search of him. "Sorry. I thought you'd gotten cold feet."

"More like bloody," she groused.

He scooped her up in his arms and carried her back to his bedroom. "It's your own fault. If you hadn't been such a chicken, we'd be in bed by now."

She punched his shoulder. "I'm *not* a chicken. I needed to use my hair dryer."

"I *have* one in this bathroom, too, you know. Be honest. You got scared in the shower."

His chest was warm and hard beneath her cheek. He held her with disarming ease, not even breathing heavily.

"Maybe a little," she admitted. "But that doesn't mean I don't want you."

"That's verra good," he said, looking down at her with a feral masculine grin that curled her aching toes. He dropped her on the mattress. "Don't move. I'll get supplies."

She held up her foot, loathe to get blood on the very nice comforter. "It's not really so bad. More of a scrape than a cut."

Duncan returned and sat down on the bed, lifting her leg across his lap. "Let me take a look." He dabbed at the blood with an alcohol wipe. "I think two tiny Band-Aids will do it."

Abby screeched. "That stings."

"Quit bein' such a wee bairn. Hold still." He spread antibiotic ointment across the two toes with the worst abrasions and covered them. "All done." His thumb pressed the arch of her foot. "Do you hurt anywhere else, lass?"

Abby fell back on her elbows. Unfortunately, that made the sides of her robe gape. "My lips could use a kiss," she whispered. "You know. 'Cause they went numb when I was looking at this huge, gorgeous, naked man a little while ago."

Duncan's gaze locked on to her breasts. His pupils dilated. "I understand." Lazily, as if he had all the time in the world, he tossed the towel aside, flipped back the covers and dragged Abby between the sheets with him.

The cool cotton made her shiver.

They rolled together in a delicious tangle of arms and legs and fractured breaths. "Duncan," she said, suddenly fixating on the one question she had never asked. "Is there a woman back in Skye who might have a problem with what's happening between us?"

He had been about to kiss her, but now he froze and reared back, a frown creasing his noble brow. "No. And if there *had* been anyone like that, I'd have ended it before I left. Would no' have been fair to ask a lass to wait for me when I thought I was coming here to stay."

"I suppose that's true."

"Do you always talk this much during sex?" he asked, grinning to let her know he was teasing.

Abby sniffed. "If you'd kissed me already, I wouldn't have been able to talk, now would I?"

Duncan was more than a little infatuated with his sharp-tongued, quick-witted Abby. She was fierce and caring, and now that he had her naked again, he was done with conversation for the moment.

He took her chin in one hand, tilted it up and captured her mouth roughly, nipping her bottom lip with sharp teeth. She tasted like sweet honey and feminine temptation.

Taking his time with her, he gave her every nuance he'd been too obliterated the night before to offer. Coaxing, persuading, insisting. She met him taste for taste, ragged sigh for ragged sigh. When had merely kissing a woman ever made his entire body ache with need?

He had let her keep the sexy robe for a moment, but now he wanted it gone so he could taste and touch and torment her lush, beautiful breasts. With his teeth and his tongue and his fingertips, he played and cajoled and teased. Her nipples were pert, rigid raspberries. Her curves were a man's playground, warm and full and sensitive to his touch.

But other delights awaited.

Before Abby could think to protest, he slipped the narrow sash from her robe and anchored her wrists at the spindled headboard. Her eyes widened. "What are you doing, Duncan?"

"Dinna fash yerself, lass. I've a mind to play. But you can stop me anytime. Do you understand?" He gazed at her for long seconds, letting her see the full extent of his hunger, but also telling her with more than mere words that he would keep her safe.

Whatever she saw in his eyes must have reassured her. "I understand, Duncan. You're the boss."

She said the last three words deliberately. Nothing in their relationship to date had been about Abby taking a subservient role. She was a smart, well-educated woman who was the equal of any man. Her sly comment indicated that she was willing to play his game.

Hearing those three words in the context of this sexual encounter snapped the tight control he had kept on his libido. Abby was naked and willing in his bed. Tonight, he would not let her go.

He slid a bit lower on the mattress and deliberately parted her legs. The scent of damp female skin and shower soap filled his lungs. He traced the crease where her leg joined her body. "Sometimes a man likes dessert *before* his dinner."

Abby actually cried out when he tasted her intimately. Her thighs tightened around him, but he kept her legs spread. The sight of her moist folds, ready for him, sent his arousal up a thousand fold. He ran his tongue over her sex lazily, hitting the most sensitive spot and then bit her inner thigh when she climaxed wildly. "Untie me," she cried.

He rested his cheek on her trembling thigh as she came down from the top. "I dinna think I will. Unless you really mean that. Do you want me to stop, Abby?"

Her chest rose and fell rapidly. Her entire body was one pink blush. Her gaze couldn't quite meet his. He had never seen a more erotic, sensual tableau of abandon.

She swallowed visibly. "No, Duncan. Don't stop."

He went a little crazy after that. He made her come twice more in a similar fashion until he allowed her to recover and catch her breath. It seemed best to take a linear approach next so he shoved *all* the covers back and nibbled her perfectly pink-polished toes.

Abby was ticklish at first. But when he took her toes one at a time and suckled them, she didn't seem to mind.

After that, he kissed his way up her shapely calves, pausing to nip the insides of her knees, before returning to her female secrets.

Again, she tried to close her legs. He gripped her ankles firmly. "Don't try to thwart me, Abby. You said I'm the boss. I know very well what you want. It's the same thing I want. Do I need to tie your feet apart to make you behave?"

"No," she said quickly, her breath coming in sharp pants. "Don't do that. I'll behave. I promise."

He nodded slowly. "Excellent." Her faux submissive dialogue went straight to his gut and kept him on a slow boil.

Abby watched him with trepidation in her wide-eyed gaze. He wanted to laugh, but he was having too much fun and he didn't want to ruin the mood.

When he stood up, she dug her heels into the mattress, alarm on her face. "Why are you leaving?"

"Nothing so dreadful, sweet Abby. Close your eyes and rest."

"Fat chance," she muttered.

He was gone less than two minutes. When he returned, Abby's eyes were closed, but her body was rigid. He stroked her hair. "This next bit will go easier if you can't see what I'm doing."

At his matter-of-fact words, Abby struggled wildly. But the knots at her wrists held firm. Her robe was made of a thin fabric that was almost transparent... almost, but not quite. Artfully, he arranged it over the top of her face, taking care not to cover her nose.

He tapped her chin. "Is it dark in there, lass?"

She nodded her head slowly.

"Do you want me to stop?"

Her silence lasted eons, it seemed. He'd given her multiple orgasms. His own erection ached like the devil, but he was not anywhere close to being done with Abby Hartmann. He waited impatiently for her answer.

"No," she whispered. "I don't want you to stop."

"Good girl." The words were gruff with arousal and pleasure and a rush of affection for this woman who had given him so much in such a short time. "You won't regret your answer, I swear."

Nine

Abby had unwittingly unleashed a monster. Duncan Stewart was the most sexually uninhibited man she had ever encountered. When she said as much, he scoffed. "It's not me, lass, it's you. I've been corrupted by a wicked American siren."

Since she was momentarily blind, she couldn't see his face, but she could hear the smirk in his voice. It was when he got quiet that she really worried.

For several long moments, she was aware that he had left the bedroom again. But this time, he hadn't gone far. She could hear water running and the sound of drawers opening and closing in the bathroom.

At last, she felt the mattress give as he joined her. Without realizing she was doing it, she jerked at her bonds. Duncan only laughed, damn his hide. "Patience, my little Venus. I won't make you wait much longer."

Abby wasn't sure what she had expected him to do next. After all, there were only a finite number of ways a man and a woman could make love…right?

And even a Scotsman descended from a long line of occasionally barbaric Highlanders would be completely civilized *now*. Even so, her skin was covered in gooseflesh, and her heart pounded so hard in her chest she could barely breathe. The waiting was excruciating.

Duncan smoothed her hair, toying with the shell of her ear. "Why are you so tense, sweet Abby?"

"You know why," she said tartly. "You're tormenting me deliberately."

"Shall I stop?"

His question was bland. Conversational in tone.

She ground her jaw. Despite the recent orgasms, her body was wound so tightly she craved his touch like a drug. "Just do it," she said desperately. "Do whatever it is you're going to do."

When he touched her hip bone, she jerked and cried out.

Duncan murmured something she didn't quite catch. "Poor Abby. You're imagining the worst, aren't you?"

"Maybe that's because I don't really know you at all." It was a fact. That one inescapable truth should have bothered her more than it did.

He laughed softly. "You know me well enough, I'd say. As well as I know you. We see something in each other, lass. Maybe something that no one else sees. And we're curious."

She licked her dry lips. He wasn't wrong. "I trust you for some odd reason. And I don't know why."

"Mystical connections defy explanation. We Scots don't have a problem with that. Life offers rare gifts sometimes, even when we least expect them."

He ran a finger from her chin, down her throat, between her breasts and all the way to her navel where he played lazily. "I want to devour you, Abby. It gives me pause, to be sure. I've no' been quite so consumed with lust since I was teenager."

The words poured over her like fire that heated from the inside out. She wanted to hold him and cling to him and force him to take her, but she had committed to playing this game, so she took a deep breath and braced for what was to come. "I'm all yours," she whispered.

There was silence for a moment. Perhaps her honesty stunned him. He whispered a phrase in Gaelic again. She *really* needed to learn a few of those words. And then he touched her breast.

She had expected something. She didn't know what. But this wasn't it. Earlier, he had used his teeth on the sensitive tips of her breasts to bring her to the brink of release.

This seduction was different. She felt his fingers massaging her nipples. But there was an added sensation… "Duncan?"

"Relax, lass. It's only honey. Nothing so terrible." He moved to the other breast. "I told you. Sometimes a man likes dessert first. I saw a hummingbird when we were up on the mountain. That made me think of nectar and that made me think of you. Yield to me, sweet Abby, while I enjoy my treat."

She lost herself. There was no other way to describe what happened next. Time and place drifted away until her world was filled with Duncan and only Duncan. He suckled at her breasts, groaning and shuddering as if *he* were the one being tortured, and not the other way around. The feel of his rough, insistent tongue on her aching flesh made her writhe and cry out his name again and again.

The act of helpless surrender fed her need for him to a frightening degree. She couldn't see. She could barely move. All she could do was arch and twist and lift toward him as his hot breath cooled her damp skin and he savored her honey-tipped breasts.

When she could find her voice, she pleaded. "I want to touch you, Duncan. Please. No more games."

He stopped instantly. Fumbling and cursing, he worked to free her hands. In her struggles, the slick fabric knots had tightened. It took him long, frustrating moments. Almost as an afterthought it seemed, he tugged the robe away from her face.

Their eyes met. Duncan was flushed, his expression both exultant and wary…as if he expected her to berate him.

She rotated her wrists, feeling the painful rush of blood returning fully to her chilled fingers. Lifting her aching arms, she took his face in her hands, staring deeply into his beautiful eyes. "You are a wicked, wicked man," she whispered, her throat tight with emotions that were new and terrifying. "At the risk of feeding your already considerable ego, I have to tell you I'm very, very glad you came to my office that first day. I consider you mine now. As long as your feet are on American soil."

His lips quirked in a half smile. "The bargain goes both ways, lass. You'll warm my bed and no other."

She kissed him softly, drunk with wonder that such a man had fallen into her lap. "Do we need legal paperwork?" she teased.

"No. I dinna think so. We've honesty between us, and that's all that matters."

She hesitated. He knew everything about her that was important. "I agree."

What had begun as fury and urgency and grappling for position out on the mountain now shifted seamlessly to something far sweeter and infinitely more alluring. Duncan left the bed only a moment to take care of protection and then he was back.

He kissed the side of her neck. "I can't wait any longer, Abby. I'll go mad if I don't have you now."

"I can't have that on my conscience." She didn't want Duncan to see her insecurity, so she let him take the lead. Though she had been bold in claiming him verbally, the mechanics of sexual variation were less familiar to her.

Duncan had no such handicap. Though she didn't want to think about the other women who might have shared encounters with him, it was definitely to her benefit that he had enough experience for both of them.

Oddly, Duncan appeared to have exhausted his need for *kink*, as it were. He moved between her legs, spread them wide with his powerful hips and used his hand to guide the head of his erection to her ready sex. With one firm thrust, he lodged deep. With a second, he went all the way.

"Look at me, lass. Don't close your eyes," he said.

The intimacy was painful. Her gaze clung to his. She was mute. Fearful he would realize how fast she was falling, how far, how irreversibly plunged into infatuation. Not love. Love came with time.

His jaw clenched. His brow was damp. "Ye're a wonder, Abby Hartmann. A wee, magical sprite of a woman." He flexed his hips. "Hold on, lass. I've waited too long."

He cursed in Gaelic and moved in her wildly, filling her, pummeling her, claiming her. It was insanity and exhilaration and at the end, another shattering climax. His release came fast on the heels of hers.

Collapsing on top of her, he gave her his full weight, pinning her to the bed in a deeply blissful capture.

Abby didn't mind.

"I canna feel my legs," he said. "Is that normal, do you think?"

She smiled, stroking his hair lazily. "I think we passed *normal* several stops back. Don't worry, Duncan. I'm here for you. Take as long as you need."

Duncan felt exhaustion roll over him like a seductive tide. He couldn't succumb. There was too much to do. Soon enough, he would have time to devote to Abby. But not until a grandson discharged his duty.

He recognized the danger in his current situation. Being with Abby anesthetized him, helped him to forget for a few sweet moments the weight of grief and obligation. He rolled to his side. "I suppose we should eat something."

She ran a hand lazily down his back, threatening to rekindle his interest. "Yes…." Her stomach growled on cue.

Their shared laughter was enough to propel them out of the bed. Duncan caught her close as she walked by him to go to her room. "Wear one of my shirts," he said. "I want you naked underneath." He rummaged in the closet and handed her one. The solid navy cotton was a perfect foil for her vibrant hair.

Abby took the shirt with a raised eyebrow. "Do I have permission to go to my own bathroom, sir?" She gave him a mock salute.

"You're a brat. And yes. But only because if I get you in my shower again, we'll be in trouble."

"Smart man."

He cleaned up and put on old jeans and a flannel shirt. Leaving his feet bare, he prowled the hall until she joined him. "Did you follow the rules?" he asked. The shirttail hit her just above her knees. He caught her close and ran his hands over her bottom. "Good girl."

"I'm gonna get cold."

"I'll turn up the heat."

They made their way to the kitchen, holding hands. Abby's friend and her mother had cooked so much food that Duncan and Abby were able to eat a second meal and still have some left over.

He devoured his portions. "I've always heard about the cuisine in the American South. Clearly, the stories are true. This is amazing."

"Not everyone is a great cook, though. I'm decent, but not in Lara's league. I've learned a few tricks over the years."

"Maybe you could show me a few of those tricks

later," he said, stealing a kiss flavored with cinnamon and apples.

"I was talking about food, not sex."

"We could improvise."

Suddenly, Abby blushed from her toes to her hairline, obviously remembering his honey assault. "Stop," she said, her expression mortified. "I can't talk about this at the dinner table."

He manufactured an innocent expression. "Shall we go back to bed then?"

"Duncan Stewart. Behave. We have to be sensible."

She was right. He knew it. But he didn't have to like it. "Fine," he said. He stood with a sigh and began putting things away. "But you're no fun."

When the kitchen was back to rights, she grimaced and touched his shoulder. "At the risk of spoiling your mood, I need to go to my house and get something to wear for the funeral. Lara did a great job packing, but she wouldn't have known what to bring for something like that. I could borrow your car if you don't mind. I won't be gone long."

The notion of her leaving him alone in this huge house put lead in his stomach. "What if I go with you? Is that okay? I'd like to see where you live."

Abby shrugged. "Of course it's okay. I thought you might have things to do here."

"I need to clear my head. A drive will be nice."

Unfortunately for Duncan, the current plan meant that Abby actually had to get dressed. He much preferred keeping her locked away in his castle on the hill.

The drive into town was a familiar one now. Passing the building where Stewart Properties was housed

gave him mixed emotions. Guilt. Pride. Consterna-
tion. He needed to sell the company in such a way
that people wouldn't lose their jobs. Was that even
possible?

When he pulled up in front of Abby's neat frame
bungalow, he smiled. "I've decided this house looks
like you. It's perfect."

"You wouldn't say that when the roof leaks every
third time it rains and the wiring is sputtering on its
last legs."

They walked up the front path side by side. "So
you're reminding me that an old house takes lots of
repairs. I live in the Scottish Highlands, lass. *Everything* is old, give or take."

"True." She laughed, unlocking the front door.
"But I'm also telling you that repairs are expensive.
I have to budget and prioritize them. It's an ongo-
ing process."

She waved him toward the small living room.
"Make yourself at home. I won't be long."

He caught her close and kissed the top of her head.
"I was serious about going to Asheville tomorrow
night. When the funeral is done. Will you come with
me?"

"Don't we need to get started on cleaning out your
grandmother's house? It's a huge job, Duncan. Even
if you call in professionals."

"I understand that. I do. Which is why we'll take a
break first…catch our breath after the funeral. I need
a buffer between tomorrow and everything else that's
to come. Will you go with me? Please?"

She nodded. "Of course."

"Bring something fancy to wear. A long dress.

Make it colorful, not gloomy. Granny would want me to honor her by living life to the fullest. We'll have a glass of champagne in her memory."

Abby wrapped her arms around his waist and hugged him. "I think that's a lovely idea. Give me twenty minutes. I'll grab what I need, and we can head back."

When she disappeared down the hallway, he snooped unashamedly. Her house was small and cozy. Hardwood floors gleamed. The pleasant scent of lemon furniture polish lingered in the air. The furniture was stylish and functional, but not expensive. Oddly, there were no framed pictures anywhere. Most people had family photos on display.

Abby's neat-as-a-pin house was warm—not impersonal—but it also revealed very little about her life. The most information he was able to glean about her in the short time he was alone to investigate was that she liked romantic suspense novels, and she had saved a number of her textbooks from law school.

He was perusing those titles when Abby returned, carrying a long garment bag.

"I'm done," she said.

"Your house is charming, lass."

"Thank you. Signing the mortgage for this property was one of the proudest days of my life. I worked hard to get to a place where I could support myself."

"You take your independence very seriously."

She cocked her head. "Is that a criticism?"

He returned a book to its assigned spot and shook his head. "Not at all. You must have matured early. I don't think I had your drive when I was in school."

His praise seemed to make her uncomfortable.

"Sometimes circumstances don't give a person much wiggle room."

He wanted to question that odd statement, but Abby glanced out the front window and muttered an imprecation, one that seemed completely unlike her. "Come into the kitchen. Hurry."

"What's wrong?" He followed her immediately, but he couldn't fathom her mood.

Suddenly, the doorbell rang. Abby paled, her expression haunted. "I'm not going to answer that. He'll go away."

"He who?" Duncan frowned. "Is someone bothering you?" His mind jumped immediately to jilted suitors and scary stalker clients.

"No. Nothing like that." She peeked around the corner cautiously. "It's my father. We don't get along."

Duncan's stomach tightened. Abby's entire demeanor had changed. Instead of the playful, confident woman he had come to know, now she was visibly tense and upset. "I'd be happy to go out there and tell him to go the hell away if you want me to…"

Her eyes rounded in horror. "Absolutely not. All we have to do is wait a minute. He'll give up and leave."

"Your car is parked out front," Duncan said, stating the obvious.

Abby winced. Clearly, she had forgotten that detail. "I often go out with friends. Someone might have picked me up. He'll take the hint."

Ten

Abby wanted to cry. Maybe Lara was right. Maybe a restraining order was the only way to keep her father at bay.

Everyone in Candlewick knew her family history. It wasn't something she could run away from. But no way in hell did she want Duncan to cross paths with the man who had made her life a misery.

Duncan's family might not be perfect, but they were not criminals. Abby's father knew nothing about honor and self-reliance. He had spent so much of his life dodging the law and juggling the consequences of his many slick schemes, he was an embarrassment to her.

She took one last furtive glimpse and was rewarded with a view of her father's dilapidated car driving away down the street. Thank God.

Managing a cheerful smile, though it felt like a clown mask stretching her face, she turned to Duncan, not quite able to meet his eyes. He had chosen one of her kitchen chairs and was seated, leaning the chair back on two legs. "We can go now," she said.

He took one of her hands in his. His male fingers were warm and strong. Hers were icy, trembling. Duncan brushed a hair from her cheek. "I don't like to see you like this, Abby. You're doing so much for me that I want to return the favor. Will you talk to me about him?"

Her stomach hurt. "There's nothing to tell...and nothing you or anybody can do. I hope the two of you never meet. It's for the best. You have to believe me on this one."

Duncan pulled her close in an embrace that was not at all sexual. His unspoken comfort was immeasurably wonderful. She wanted to bawl like a baby, but if she let go even the tiniest bit, she would fall to pieces. That was a humiliation she couldn't bear.

Gradually, her shaking subsided and her breathing returned to normal. She pulled back and rubbed her hands over her face. "Sorry I made such a big deal about it."

He dragged her close a second time. With her standing and Duncan seated, it was much easier for him to give her a searching stare. "You can trust me, lass. Surely you know that."

She wanted to. Badly. How wonderful it would be to hand over to Duncan every bit of her worry and despair and discomfort and know that someone else would intercede on her behalf.

Even so, she didn't want him witnessing the bloodlines she had come from. Her father's deceit made it doubly important for Abby not to let her parentage besmirch her personal honor. Duncan said he didn't like secrets, but the truth about Abby's family life was better left in the dark.

Besides, this thing with Duncan was temporary. There was no need for him to invest emotional support when he and Abby were never going to be anything more than two people having fun between the sheets.

"I know that," she said slowly. "And I do trust you. Maybe someday, when you're back in Scotland and I'm no more than a distant memory, I'll write you a long letter and tell you all about my father. Then, when you're done reading it, you can toss it into the fire."

"And how does that help you now?" he asked, his eyes shadowed and his brows narrowed in a frown.

She swallowed. "Being with you makes me happy, Duncan."

"I'm glad, but that doesn't really answer my question."

"Let's go back up the mountain. You have enough sadness in your life at the moment without worrying about mine."

In the hours that followed, Abby made a concerted effort to shake off the cloud of depression and anxiety that always followed in her father's wake. Duncan needed her. Her own issues could and should take a back seat right now.

Duncan spent some time on the phone with family. The sound of his voice carried around the house.

While he was otherwise occupied, Abby pondered her role in the upcoming funeral. She had brought two dresses with her for the somber occasion. One was a black, long-sleeved, lightweight wool, perfectly plain. She had worn it to her law school graduation, because she had finished midyear. The December commencement had been snowy and cold.

It was definitely suitable for a funeral, but tomorrow's weather was supposed to be sunny and warm. That was the problem with the advent of autumn in the South. You never knew what to expect.

She tried on the dress and stood in front of the bathroom mirror. It was nice. Expensive. Classy. But the funeral was going to be stressful. The church would be crowded. Stifling. Surely this was a bad choice.

The other option was also black, but far more casual. The crepe tank dress skimmed her body flatteringly and stopped just above the knee. The matching jacket was short and had three-quarter length sleeves. With the jewelry she had brought, it should do nicely.

If the church was extremely hot, she could always shed the jacket, though that would be a last resort.

When her decision was made, she went in search of Duncan and found him in the den. He wasn't watching TV. Instead, he had tuned the satellite radio to a classical channel. The Beethoven sonata playing was mournful, almost painful under the circumstances.

Duncan glanced up when she entered the room, but his expression was closed. It was no secret to her that he was using sexual intimacy to avoid thinking about what had happened in his life. In his place, she might have done the same. But she also knew that deferring all the guilt and pain and confusion was only a temporary solution.

She paused to kiss the top of his head. Then she curled up in a chair facing him. "Did you talk to Brody again?"

"Aye. He was checking up on me…making sure I was okay."

"And are you?"

Duncan's jaw tensed. "I want everything to go well at the funeral. I need to know that I've honored my grandmother's memory appropriately. Things are different here. Customs. Expectations."

"You've done all you can, Duncan. And you'll see…the town will turn out en masse tomorrow to pay their respects and to greet you. I'll play whatever role you want me to… I can keep my distance, or I can stand at your elbow and introduce you to the people I know."

"I'd be glad of your help."

It was an oddly formal statement from a man who had made passionate love to her a few hours before. Something about him was different, though she couldn't pinpoint the change.

"Is your brother second-guessing his decision not to come?"

"Not at all." Duncan jumped to his feet and prowled the room. "He did have some very definitive ideas, though."

"Oh?"

Duncan stood at the fireplace and stared into the empty hearth, his forearm propped on the mantel. "He and Cate want me to return to Scotland as soon as the funeral is over. Brody suggested putting one of Granny's senior managers in charge at the office. Then, in a couple of months when the baby is older and Brody can arrange for his business affairs to be covered, the three of them will come back to Candlewick with me and stay for six or eight weeks while we liquidate Stewart Properties and sell the house."

Abby's heart fell to her knees. "I see."

"It *would* be easier than doing it alone. Brody hasn't replaced me yet as CFO. My job and my office are waiting for me. There are a lot of big decisions to be made regarding the estate. Perhaps it makes sense to take things slowly."

"Is that what you want to do?" She could barely speak past the knot of hurt and dismay in her throat. She'd been under no illusions about the permanency of her relationship with Duncan Stewart. But she surely hadn't expected it to end so soon.

Duncan continued to prowl. His body language was indicative of his mental turmoil. At one point, he paused in front of the radio and jabbed the power button, filling the room with silence.

He spun to face Abby. "I don't know *what* I want," he said, the words low and taut with emotion. "When I thought my coming here was a years-long sentence, I felt trapped. Now that I'm suddenly free, it all seems different. *Sad. Final.* Grandda and Granny spent their lives building this business and this home. Who am I to toss it all away?"

"Miss Izzy wouldn't have expected you to stay once she was gone."

He ran his hands through his hair. He was pale beneath his tan. "You don't know that. *I* don't know that.

Maybe she was hoping I would become emotionally invested and keep Stewart Properties in the family."

"Even if that were true, it doesn't matter, Duncan. She lived a full and wonderful life. She *had* her dreams fulfilled. You aren't bound by anything, either legally or emotionally. As far as her will is concerned, you—and to a lesser extent Brody—have the power to call the shots. There's nothing unethical or immoral about selling out and returning to Scotland."

His gaze narrowed. "Are you being helpful and saying what you think I want to hear, or is this speech about the buyer you and your firm have waiting in the wings like a vulture?"

The sudden attack caught her off guard.

It hurt. A lot.

She lifted her chin. "You're upset. I'm going to pretend like you didn't say that." Tears threatened. "Good night, Duncan. I'll see you in the morning."

Turning her back on him, she walked away, her vision blinded by the hot rush of emotion.

She was almost out of the room when he grabbed her arm and whirled her around. "I'm sorry, damn it. I shouldn't have said that." He cupped her face in his big, warm palms and bent to look her in the eyes. "Don't cry, lass. I can't bear it. I'm a beast, I know. My head's awhirl with all manner of dreadful thoughts. Don't walk away from me. You're the only anchor in my storm."

Though Duncan did his best to make up for his appalling behavior, he knew he had hurt Abby badly. She pretended that his apology had sufficed to set things right between them, but the atmosphere in the house was definitely strained.

They watched a movie together. He had assumed Abby would spend the night in his bed. Now, he was not so sure.

At eleven, she excused herself, pleading fatigue. He wanted to follow her, but a gaping crevasse had opened up between them. Undeniably his fault.

He wanted the clock to fast-forward. He wanted the funeral to be over. He wanted to be alone with Abby at a romantic hotel tomorrow night.

Instead, he had dark, lonely hours to fill.

When it was clear that Abby was not going to change her mind and pick up where they had left off after their provocative afternoon of lovemaking, Duncan showered and climbed into bed. As soon as he turned out the lights, all his doubts and worries tripled.

Maybe Brody was right. Scotland was home. It was familiar. Perhaps a couple of months would be enough time to heal from grief and to prepare for the huge task of dismantling his grandparents' legacy.

At 2:00 a.m., sleep still eluded him. He wandered through the silent house, feeling more alone than if Abby had returned to her own place. Knowing that she was near but out of reach made his gut tight with regret. And what about his plan to escape after the funeral tomorrow? Had his outburst derailed that, as well?

Maybe he had provoked an argument, because deep down, he still mistrusted Abby's motives for staying by his side and in his bed.

He wouldn't be the first man to be manipulated by

sex. Abby was ambitious. Nothing wrong with that. She worked hard, and she had a bright future ahead of her at the law firm. Pulling off the sale of Stewart Properties for her boss would be a coup for Abby.

Was that why she was making herself indispensable to Isobel's heir?

Duncan wished like hell that he knew the truth.

His body was exhausted, but his brain ran at high speed. So many things to consider. If he gave in to Brody's urging and returned to Skye immediately, there would be no future at all for Duncan and Abby. Period. Was he ready for that?

And if he stayed, was it fair to keep seeing Abby, knowing that he had no intention of asking for anything permanent? The *only* reason to spend more time in Candlewick was to clean out the house and dispose of all the property. Abby had offered to help him. He could linger two weeks. Would that be long enough or too long?

Sometime after three, he stumbled back to his room and fell into bed. Though he did sleep after that, his dreams were unsettled.

When his alarm went off at eight, he threw an arm over his eyes and groaned. Unfortunately, though his body still craved sleep, he was wide awake now. Maybe he could get a jump-start on cleaning out his grandfather's office. He had to do *something* to pass the hours between now and the funeral.

Abby's bedroom door was closed. When he dressed and made his way to the kitchen, he found that she had made coffee. The American staple had become a crutch in these difficult days. He filled a cup, added some milk and went in search of his houseguest.

He found her outside on the front porch, perched on a wooden bench, enjoying the frosty morning.

She looked up when he joined her and gave him a small smile. "Did you sleep?"

"Not as well as I would have if you'd been in my bed."

He tossed it out there deliberately, hoping to gauge her mood.

She gave him a long stare and then buried her face in her cup again. Finally, she sighed. "I think your brother is probably right. I checked flights for this evening. If you head to Asheville as soon as the service is over, you can fly out and make your connection in Atlanta. You could be home by morning."

"Are you trying to get rid of me?" He propped his hip against the porch rail and scowled.

Abby nodded slowly. "If that's what you want to call it. You need some time, Duncan. Time to get your feet back under you. Having Isobel die so suddenly was a terrible shock. You don't really know *what* you want. Guilt and grief are clouding your judgment."

"So now you're a lawyer *and* a shrink?" He didn't like being psychoanalyzed any more than the next guy.

"I'm only trying to help."

"If you wanted to help me, you'd be naked right now."

Her face turned pink. "I think you're using sex to avoid your problems."

"What's wrong with that?" He was half-serious.

Abby set her cup aside, stood and stretched. The

tiny glimpse he got of her smooth belly gave him ideas. She sighed. "Why don't you show me a couple of the other guest rooms? We have a few hours to kill. I'd like to know what I'll be in for if I end up helping you."

Clearly, Abby wasn't prepared to forgive him yet. At least not enough to climb back into bed. That was okay. He could wait. Maybe.

"Fine," he said, feeling grumpy and sleep-deprived. "If you want to be overwhelmed and depressed *before* we even get to the funeral, by all means."

Fortunately, Abby seemed willing to overlook his ill humor. He led the way to one of the three guest rooms not currently in use. "We'll start with this one. Everything needs to go. Draperies, bedding." He threw open a closet. "And look at this. We've got several decades of clothing hanging here. Some of it may be rotting away, it's so old."

"Do you want to try and sell it to a vintage shop somewhere?"

"I do not. My plan is to get rid of everything that won't be worth including in an estate sale. All of it goes to charity. Or the rubbish bin, if necessary."

Abby nodded, rifling through the hangers. "But I might point out that old people have a tendency to stash stuff everywhere. Checking for valuables in pockets and drawers and everything in between will slow things down considerably."

"I suppose." The subject couldn't hold his attention. Not with Abby right in front of him.

He was close enough to indulge his impulses. Lifting a lock of her hair, he rubbed it between his fingers. "I appreciate your efforts on my behalf, Abby, but I'm not going to fly back to Scotland tonight. You promised to go away with me and celebrate Granny Isobel's life."

"That's what a funeral is for."

The words were snippy, but he took heart in the fact that she didn't step away. "Please, lass." He brushed a kiss over the back of her nape, smiling inwardly when she shivered. She might be mad at him, but she wasn't indifferent. "You and me," he coaxed. "Dinner. Dancing. A big, comfortable bed with soft sheets and breakfast in bed."

"You told me I could have my own room."

He nipped the shell of her ear with his teeth. "I lied."

She turned and held him at bay with a hand planted in the middle of his chest. Big, beautiful gray eyes looked up at him searchingly. "You're giving me emotional whiplash, Duncan."

He winced. Her complaint was spot-on. He was acting like a lunatic. Amorous one minute, angry and discontent the next. "In my defense, I'm not usually so volatile. My mates call me stodgy on occasion."

Abby shook her head disbelievingly. "I doubt that. Before Miss Izzy died, you struck me as extremely grounded. Unsure of this transatlantic move, perhaps, but definitely your own man."

"You're not going to have sex with me this morning, are you?" He said it with some resignation, recognizing that *he* had been the one to cause disharmony between them.

"No," she said firmly. "I'm not. We have several hours until we have to leave for the funeral. I think it would be best if we each tackle separate rooms."

He rubbed his thumb over her cheekbone. "And after the funeral? Are you still willing to go away with me?"

She chewed her bottom lip. "For one night only. We come home Monday evening. Agreed? You have decisions to make, possibly even travel arrangements."

"Fine," he said, wishing he had bartered for two nights from the beginning. Abby had the end of their relationship in view, and he didn't want to admit she might be right. He didn't want to let her go. "One night. I'll make it count." The sick feeling in the pit of his stomach told him this temporary affair was going to be far shorter than he had ever imagined.

Eleven

Later that day, Abby fetched a cup of water and as unobtrusively as possible, handed it to Duncan. He accepted the drink with a grateful, intimate smile, downed it quickly, and turned back to his duties in the receiving line with almost no interruption. He'd been on his feet doing this for an hour already, yet the line was still out the door and down the sidewalk.

He was dressed simply but elegantly in a hand-tailored black suit that fit his tall, athletic frame perfectly. The only note of color about his appearance was a jaunty red bow tie. He had insisted that his grandmother wouldn't have wanted everything today to be doom and gloom, so he had worn the pop of crimson in her honor.

Abby leaned in and whispered quietly. "The next

couple is the mayor and his wife. She owns the local diner."

Duncan didn't miss a beat. He greeted the man and woman with a warm smile and words of thanks for their presence. Abby didn't know if it was the Scottish accent, or the combo of tall, dark and handsome, or simply the fact that curiosity had won out, but it seemed that everyone in town had come to pay their respects to Isobel Stewart and to extend condolences to her extraordinarily charismatic grandson.

Duncan had decided on an open casket. Miss Isobel looked sweet and serene as people filed past her with tears and smiles. Abby suspected that the spirited old woman would have been mightily pleased.

Geoffrey and Isobel had been longtime members of the First Presbyterian Church of Candlewick. The church was small. Well-worn wooden pews provided seating for eighty worshippers, maybe a hundred if folks squeezed together.

The turnout for today's funeral service was well over twice that number. Mourners were being seated in the choir loft and in a series of folding metal chairs rapidly produced from some other area of the church.

Fortunately, the building did not have ornate stained glass windows. The smaller, tinted-glass panes opened outward to catch the afternoon breeze. Even so, the sanctuary was sweltering. Though the obituary had requested donations be made to charity in lieu of flowers, the entire staff of Stewart Properties had pitched in together for an enormous arrangement of bronze and golden-yellow mums, Miss Izzy's favorite flowers.

The service was slated to begin in less than thirty

minutes. Soon, the funeral home staff would begin courteously but firmly cutting off the line so that Duncan could take his place for the service. Abby did not feel entirely comfortable about the prospect of being seated in the front row beside him.

Her position at his elbow had elicited stares and hushed, gossipy whispers. She bore the scrutiny with as much grace as she could. Today was about Duncan and his comfort and well-being. Abby's reputation could handle the fallout.

When there were only a handful of people still waiting to speak to Isobel's grandson, she made a mad dash for the restroom. On her way out, she ran into Lara.

Her friend gave her a hug. "Well," she said, pulling back to gaze at Abby's face. "Is it bad form to say you look sexy in that dress?"

Abby tugged her toward a back hallway. "Ssshhh. Don't give the biddies more fodder. Talking to poor Duncan is the most excitement they've had in months."

"Well, at least since his brother, Brody, knocked up the bookstore lady and married her."

"Those Stewart boys *do* know how to make an impression."

Abby spoke lightly, but Lara knew her too well to be fooled. Her eyes rounded. "You're sleeping with him, aren't you!"

"For heaven's sake, keep your voice down."

"I don't know whether to be proud or jealous. One of you is a fast worker."

Abby shrugged with a wry smile. "I may have taken *cheering him up* a little too far."

"Abby Hartmann. You're a bad girl. Who knew? I don't know what to say."

"Very funny. It just happened. Neither of us planned it."

Lara sobered. "He's not going to stay now, is he? Now that Isobel is dead?"

"Probably not." Abby made herself say the words out loud. "I've offered to help him tackle cleaning out the house...or at least the preparations before a team of professionals comes in."

"Why?"

Lara's blunt question exposed the weaknesses in Abby's self-destructive rationalizations. "I feel sorry for him," she muttered.

"The man is a millionaire several times over. I'm pretty sure he can hire whoever he needs."

"That's cold even for you, Lara. Show some compassion. His grandmother just died."

"And yet he's already coaxed you into his bed."

"It wasn't like that." Abby stopped, suddenly unwilling to justify her behavior. She didn't want to talk about Duncan's grief on the night they found Izzy. What had happened between Duncan and Abby was natural and organic. She wouldn't let that memory be sullied by Lara's understandable cynicism. "I have to go," she said. "It's time for the service."

Lara hugged her again, her expression contrite. "You're a good person. I hope Duncan knows how lucky he is to have you."

Lara's words played again and again in Abby's head during the lengthy service. She didn't think Duncan meant for it to be so long, but he had made the choice to open up the eulogy time for anyone who wanted to say a few words about Isobel. There were many who seized the opportunity to speak about a woman who had done so much and left such a lasting impression.

At last, after a soloist sang one more song, Duncan stepped forward to conclude the remarks.

He cleared his throat. "My grandparents were part of a generation who believed in hard work and family. They raised my father to be self-reliant, and when Brody and I came along, they extended those lessons to us, as well. This town and this community meant the world to them. Candlewick will always be part of the Stewart legacy. Thank you for coming here today. On behalf of all my family, I appreciate the honor you have shown my grandmother."

And then it was over.

The crowd filed out one cluster at a time. After the minister spoke to Duncan briefly, there were a few more well-wishers waiting for his attention.

Abby slipped away to stand beside the casket. "Godspeed, Miss Izzy," she whispered. "He did well, didn't he?" Duncan's words had left no room for misinterpretation. He was saying *thank you* and *goodbye*. When he talked about Candlewick *always* being part of the Stewart legacy, there had been a note of finality in his voice.

Duncan might be conflicted about his inheritance, but it was painfully clear to Abby that his presence in North Carolina was brief, at best.

When the crowd finally dispersed, Duncan took Abby's hand and gripped it tightly. They walked out the back of the church to the small cemetery where

Isobel's spot beside her husband had been prepared. Duncan stood straight and tall, but she could read the strain on his face.

The minister read a scripture and said a prayer. Abby and Duncan put two flowers on the casket. Then the little woman was lowered to her final resting place.

Duncan sighed deeply and put an arm around Abby's waist. "Was it okay?" he asked, his expression sober.

"It was perfect."

He nodded. "Good."

The minister shook Duncan's hand. "The ladies of the church want to prepare a meal for you this coming Tuesday. They weren't sure of your plans, so they've asked me to make sure that's a convenient time."

"Of course. Please tell them thank you. I appreciate their kindness."

"I'll drop it by your house around noon."

When the older man disappeared, Duncan rotated his neck. "I'm exhausted," he muttered.

"Are you sure you still want to go to Asheville?"

"I don't want to go alone," he said.

Abby straightened his bow tie for an excuse to touch him. "I'll go with you. You knew I would."

"On the contrary," he said. "I'm not sure of anything about you, Abby. But I'm willing to learn."

Duncan was so tired his eyeballs hurt. The last hours had been an endurance test. His face hurt from smiling and pretending to be *okay*, whatever that meant. Deeper still was the unexpectedly sharp sting of grief. Seeing the raw earth accept his grand-mother's casket had shaken him.

Maybe taking Abby to a luxurious hotel for an overnight getaway was a bloody stupid idea, but he clung to it like a life raft. If he could get her there and get her naked and in his arms, he might be able to sleep tonight.

They arrived at the Gloucester Park Inn at six. The stately four-story building was a local landmark. He barely remembered the drive. Abby had been quiet beside him, and he had concentrated on the direc-tions from his phone. He handed the valet his keys and went to check in.

When he returned, Abby stood beside their two small suitcases. "I told the bellman we didn't need help," she said. "I didn't think you would mind."

"Of course not." He was running on adrenaline, and his nerves were jumpy. Having a third person around, even momentarily, would not help the situa-tion. Abby's mood was impossible to read. "Let's go upstairs," he said.

Their room, actually a suite, was on the top floor of the hotel. Duncan had paid extra for a view of the mountains and a welcome basket of champagne and cheese and strawberries.

Abby kicked off her heels immediately and went to the bay window. "This is gorgeous," she said. She looked over her shoulder at him and smiled. "I've al-ways heard about this place."

He joined her and slid his arms around her from behind. "I like this western part of North Carolina. It reminds me a little bit of home."

"Except no water."

"Aye. That's true." He nuzzled her ear. "Did you bring the fancy dress?"

"I did."

"Then go change and we'll open that champagne. Our dinner reservations are at seven, so we don't have too much time to spare."

"I'm not high maintenance," Abby said, slipping out of his embrace. "It won't take me long."

The beautifully decorated suite was spacious. In addition to the sitting room where they had first entered that included multiple sofas and love seats, there was an enormous bedroom and bathroom. Perhaps in deference to family groups who might book the facilities, there was a smaller nook with a full bath in one corner of the living area.

Duncan could hear the shower running in the other room, so he knew Abby was freshening up. Suddenly, that sounded like a fantastic idea. He took his suitcase into the miniature bathroom and followed her example.

He'd brought an entire change of clothes for tonight. Not only was he hot and rumpled, but he wanted to symbolically shed his funeral attire. Life was made up of beginnings and endings. Today had been one.

Was tonight a beginning? Or simply another ending?

The thought tormented him, so he pushed it away.

When Abby walked out of the bedroom at twenty 'til seven, she took his breath away. Her gorgeous hair fluffed out in a sexy halo around her head. Her makeup was more dramatic than usual, smoky eyes and pouty lips.

But it was the dress that made his mouth dry and his heart pound. Her curvaceous body was show-cased in fire-engine red sequins that caught the light when she walked. Tiny spaghetti straps bared white shoulders.

The bodice plunged dramatically, making it clear that his pragmatic Abby had dispensed with a bra. Her curvy hips begged for a man's touch.

"My God," he said reverently. "You look like a film star."

"You're not so bad yourself." She went up on her tiptoes and kissed his cheek. "And you smell yummy."

"I showered, too. We should have done it together and saved water."

"Not a chance, Duncan. I know where that would have ended up. You promised me dinner and danc-ing."

He grinned at her, feeling some of the weight in his chest ease. "Aye, I did." He reached for the cham-pagne and popped the cork. Carefully, he filled two flutes and handed one to Abby. "A toast tonight. To Isobel Stewart, my stubborn, feisty grandmother. May she and her Geoffrey be together always."

Abby touched her glass to his with a wistful smile. "A lovely thought." She took a sip of the bubbly and sneezed.

Duncan laughed and drained his glass. "That's damned fine champagne."

While he stared, Abby sipped hers slowly. "Don't," she said.

"Don't what?"

"Don't look at me like you're the big bad wolf and I'm dinner."

"I can't help it," he said. It was the truth. "I can't take my eyes off of you."

She set her empty glass aside and tugged at the bodice. "I think I've gained a couple of pounds since the last time I wore this. I don't remember it being quite so..."

"Glorious? Incandescent? Ravishing?"

Her expression was an odd mixture of pleasure and disbelief. "I thought it was Irish men who kissed the blarney stone."

"If I were going to stick around for any length of time, I'd prove to you how beautiful you are."

A heartbeat passed. Then two. "If you were going to stick around, I might let you."

Duncan felt a shift between them, a bittersweet acknowledgment that they had come close to having something special. The prospect of leaving Abby was physically painful. It was a reality he would have to address, but not tonight, not now.

"Let's head downstairs," he said gruffly.

The dining room of the Gloucester Park Inn was black-tie only. Its centerpiece was an enormous antique chandelier that cast light in a million rainbows across the elegant space. Beneath was a highly polished dance floor. Dinner tables, staggered several deep, ran around all four sides of the rectangular room. French doors opened out onto a terraced patio for use when weather permitted.

Duncan had requested a corner table that afforded a modicum of privacy.

Abby's obvious enthusiasm pleased him. "I see now what all the hype was about," she said. "No wonder couples save their pennies for a night out."

"Indeed." The crowd was eclectic, but no children in sight.

The waiter arrived and handed them menus. Abby studied hers with charming seriousness. "I believe I'll have the salmon and asparagus," she said.

Duncan decided to try the prime Angus steak. When they had ordered, he held out his hand, no longer willing to wait. "Let's dance."

Abby's beaming smile warmed him to his toes. "I thought you'd never ask."

He led her out onto the dance floor, ruefully conscious that his height and hers did not make for perfect partners. Nevertheless, he folded her into his arms, smiling when her cheek rested over his heart. She had worn sexy shoes with stiletto heels that gave her an additional three inches.

Although dancing was not Duncan's usual recreation, he knew enough to pilot his partner around the dance floor. A six-piece orchestra played beautiful evocative melodies. He closed off the memories of the past week and concentrated on Abby. The music soothed him.

He inhaled her delicate scent. In his embrace, she felt soft and warm and intensely feminine. It was impossible to imagine walking away from this unexpected, visceral connection. And yet what did he really know about her? The woman scarcely talked about herself at all. Was she simply reserved or intentionally secretive?

If Duncan remained in Candlewick, there might be a chance for the two of them, but every time he contemplated staying, his stomach tightened with panic.

Taking Abby to Scotland was no better plan. She

had worked hard to get where she was in her career. Starting over in Skye would be virtually impossible.

He splayed his fingers over her bare back, shuddering inwardly as he imagined having her naked again. His body responded predictably. Since he still had to make it through dinner, he reached desperately for something to distract himself. "Tell me about your family," he said. "You know everything about me."

Abby stiffened in his embrace. Noticeably. He felt the tension in her body. It made no sense. "Abby?" he prodded.

Her fingers were white-knuckled at the breast pocket of his jacket. "Not much to tell," she said. The words were nonchalant, her tone anything but.

"Your mother must have been a beautiful woman. I'm assuming you look like her?"

She made a sound in her throat that might have been agreement or denial. "Sometimes I think I have a snippet of a memory, but it might be my imagination. I have a few photographs. She was a teacher before I was born."

"How did she die?"

"Her appendix ruptured. She let it go too long before she went to the doctor. The infection caused sepsis."

He stroked her hair. "It's not right for a bairn to grow up without her mum. I'm sorry you lost yours."

"Thank you."

"You haven't said much about your father."

"And I won't." The words were sharp.

There was a story there, and not a pleasant one, it seemed. "I won't force it out of you. But if you and he don't get along, why have you stayed here? 'Tis a lovely town, for sure. Still, there would have been more opportunities in a bigger city. You're smart and ambitious. What keeps you in Candlewick?"

Abby looked up at him, her gray eyes dark with mysteries he couldn't fathom. "My mother is buried here. I often go to her grave and talk to her about my life. It's not morbid, I swear." Her lopsided smile was self-deprecating. "It makes me happy to think she might be proud of me."

"I'd say that's a fair bet. Ye've done well for yourself, Abby Hartmann."

It was true. For a young woman with little parental support as far as he could tell, Abby had accomplished a lot in her short life. He had witnessed her devotion to her boss's cause. If she was as doggedly determined in *every* arena of her life, Abby might end up running the law firm one day.

Why did the notion bother him so much? He should be happy for her.

The song ended and Abby stepped away from him, smoothing her hair. "Our food is here," she said. "I'm starving. Do you mind?"

"Of course not."

The easy communication between them had been shattered. Duncan marked it to the moment he asked about her father. Abby was keeping something from him. Perhaps it wasn't his business, but her reticence brought more questions than answers.

Twelve

Duncan's innocent questions about her family had erased most of Abby's pleasure in the evening. If theirs was a serious relationship, she would perhaps be obliged to share all the sordid details of her family tree. But this fling, or whatever it was, had *temporary* written all over it. She had no interest in telling Duncan all her secrets.

It was bad enough that he had almost met her father. The incident at her house had embarrassed her deeply and reminded her of all the reasons why she should watch her step around Duncan. He was a client of the law firm that had taken a chance on her, given her a job, kept her from starving in the streets. She was risking her professional integrity by socializing with someone whose business interests were inextricably intertwined with her livelihood. Candlewick was a small town. If Abby made a misstep in her personal life that had implications for her career, everyone would know.

When their food arrived, they ate mostly in silence. The meal was astonishingly good. Abby was hungry. Or at least she had been earlier. Now, the knot in her stomach made it difficult to eat more than a portion of her beautifully prepared food.

Fortunately, Duncan didn't comment. He cleaned his plate and downed two glasses of wine. Abby drank sparingly. She was nervous, but she wanted to go into the intimacies of the night with a clear head. Maybe she *was* a control freak. But that bent had served her well.

She would have skipped dessert, but Duncan ordered the special without consulting her. The cinnamon and fruit crisp was made from fresh local apples and topped with vanilla ice cream. The scent and taste of the cobbler brought home the flavors of autumn.

Fall had always been a favorite season of hers, but the cooler days and longer nights were not without melancholy, especially now. Winters in the mountains came early and could be harsh, depending on the year. Duncan would likely be long gone before the Christmas season. And in his leaving, he would take all the joy and the color with him.

For one bleak moment, she wished desperately that she had never met him at all. Not when the outcome was foretold with such dismal certainty.

He scooped up the last bite and offered it to her, waiting for her mouth to open. She swallowed the sweet dessert and tried not to let him see how much his casual gesture affected her.

No matter how many times she told herself he was leaving, a tiny flicker of hope remained. Perhaps he would decide to stay. Maybe he would ask her to go with him. It was a pleasant daydream, but one with little root in reality. Duncan still mistrusted her motives for wanting him to sell the property. It was possible he even thought she was in a relationship with him to further her career, though to any woman, such an idea was laughable. Beyond that, he had almost certainly taken offense at her unwillingness to discuss her father. Duncan knew she was keeping secrets. He wasn't stupid. And now…very soon… he would be leaving. They hadn't had time to build the kind of relationship that could withstand a physical separation. If Miss Izzy hadn't died…

Duncan lifted a hand for the check and the waiter appeared as if by magic. The Scotsman was a compelling figure in a room filled with other, lesser men. The comparison probably wasn't fair. Abby's judgment had been compromised. Tonight, she had eyes only for her dark, brooding Highlander.

He reached across the table and took her hand in his. "Upstairs?" he asked, his voice little more than a hoarse rumble.

She nodded slowly. "Yes."

When they reached the suite, her nerves increased a thousandfold. She wanted to appear sophisticated and at ease. At the moment, those attributes were as far away as the moon.

Duncan toyed with the strap of her dress, his warm fingers stroking her collarbone. "You're jittery, lass. Why?"

His plain speaking demanded an honest response.

"I like you, Duncan. And I care about you. But I don't want to have my heart broken."

Was it her imagination, or did he go pale beneath his tan? "Is that a possibility?"

She looked up at him, her smile wry. "Well, look at you. You're tall and smart and handsome as sin, and you have a wicked sense of humor. I'm not immune."

He ran the back of his hand across her cheek, his expression hard to read. "I'm not immune either. I wish our timing were better."

Even now, he acknowledged the truth of the matter. They were too new to survive his leaving. But the sexual attraction was strong.

Somewhere, she found the courage to ask the next question. "Are you going to sell the business?"

He grimaced. "Probably."

She nodded, feeling the sting of disappointment. Doggedly, she shoved the emotion aside and concentrated on the moment. "We may not have forever, Duncan, but we have tonight. Why don't you show me how a Scotsman seduces a lady?"

"That I can do," he said. His expression lightened, and in a heartbeat, the mood went from wistful to carnal. He dragged the straps of her dress down her shoulders, trapping her arms at her sides. Her breasts, unconfined by a bra, spilled out into the light. Duncan looked as if he had been poleaxed, though he had seen her naked now on multiple occasions. "Damn, you're glorious," he muttered, cupping her pale flesh in his slightly rough palms.

She had never considered her breasts as particularly sensitive. But with Duncan holding them and playing with them, her skin tightened and she shuddered inwardly. He was confident and sure. Seeing his tanned fingers against her white skin was unbearably erotic.

Her legs trembled. Her temperature skyrocketed. Her throat dried. She wriggled, trying to free her arms. "We could go to the bedroom," she said. They had made it only as far as the sitting area.

Duncan thumbed her nipples, sending streaks of fire throughout her body. His touch was both familiar and agitating. Her hunger for him eclipsed her need for self-preservation. Tonight she would give him whatever he asked.

Scooping her up in his arms, he strode through the doorway into the inner chamber. The bed was a king, miles across and laden with a dozen pristine pillows. The remainder of the champagne was still chilled. She didn't care. The soft sheets beckoned. Her head rested on Duncan's shoulder. Beneath the veneer of civilization, she felt the pounding of his heart.

"Don't make me wait," she whispered. "I want you."

Her words galvanized him. With one hand, he tore back the covers. Unceremoniously, he dumped her on the bed and came down beside her. Instead of undressing her further, he kissed her wildly, one large muscled thigh pinning her to the bed. His firm masculine lips tasted of apples. His tongue found hers and stroked it coaxingly.

No other man she had ever known had managed to take her from trembling uncertainty to unabashed arousal so quickly. Her body quivered. Her breath came and went in her lungs so rapidly, she risked hyperventilation.

Clumsily, she tugged at his jacket. He shrugged out of it without breaking the kiss. His desperation was no less than hers. They struggled and strained against each other as if determined to share the same space.

It was no beautifully choreographed ballet, but their mad dash toward nudity was effective. Soon, they were both bare-assed naked and entwined in each other's arms. Duncan's body was hard and warm and unequivocally masculine. The shape of his sex, thick and jutting, probed her hip.

She had never had any particular leaning toward men in Scottish attire, but suddenly her heart beat faster at the mental image of Duncan wearing a full dress kilt. Or even sweaty and rumpled in a working tartan. His thighs were powerful, his body tanned and lightly covered with dark hair.

Something about him was different than the men she had known. He was strong, but other men were strong, too. Perhaps it was his intensity. Duncan's ability to give laser focus to the matter at hand, whether it be sex or anything else, made him irresistible to a woman who had spent her life zeroing in on a single goal.

She had tried so hard to rise above her father's shortcomings as a parent and as a man. Nothing else had mattered to her for the longest time. Her entire focus had revolved around the need to make something of herself.

Now here she was, with a great job, a good reputation and a close circle of friends. But the one thing she wanted most of all was going to slip through her fingers. Truthfully, she hadn't known she needed a man. Things in her world had been clicking along pretty well.

Meeting Duncan had opened her eyes to what she was missing.

He bent over and licked her navel. "I think you left me, lass."

"I'm right here," she protested.

"Aye, but your attention wandered."

It amazed her that he was so attuned to her mood. No man should have that much knowledge of the feminine psyche. It made him dangerous. She cupped his head in her hands and massaged his scalp. His hair was thick and silky soft beneath her fingertips. "My apologies." Her breath caught when he moved lower and kissed her thigh. "Duncan?"

He held her down with ease and probed her intimately with his talented tongue. "Trust me, Abby. I've got you. For once, sweet girl, relax and let the moment take you."

She tried. She really did. But this level of intimacy was still relatively new ground for her. Her sexual history prior to meeting Duncan had been brief and unexceptional. Conventional. Situations where she had been in control. She liked it that way.

Sex with Duncan was different.

He demanded complete capitulation, total trust.

It wasn't easy.

Closing her eyes helped.

Her body went lax with pleasure and then climbed a sharp peak. "Enough," she cried, suddenly terrified of what he wanted from her.

He lifted one of her legs over his shoulder. "Easy, lass. What are you afraid of, sweet Abby? Let me do this for you. Ye're turning me inside out. I'm so hard I ache. Your sex is pink and swollen. I'm going to take you wild and fast and easy and slow and every way in between."

His naughty words combined with the touch of his hands and his tongue to take her deeper and further than she had ever gone with *any* man. The shattering intimacy was both terrifying and exhilarating. Then Duncan stopped talking and finished her destruction.

The peak, when it came, snatched her from complacency and threw her into a storm of pleasure so pure and hot she whimpered and gasped and cried out. "Duncan…"

He held her close as her body shivered through every last ripple. "That's my girl," he said softly. "I'm here, Abby. I'm right here."

Duncan was losing it. He had promised Abby to protect her, but what he felt at the moment was a raw, unbridled urge to take and take and take. Her body was a siren luring him to disaster. How could he want her so much and simply walk away? His brain shut down. The future was not important. All that mattered right now was how fast he could get inside her.

Fumbling and clumsy, he reached for his pants and found the condoms he had stashed in his pocket earlier. Since meeting Abby, the prospect of sex had filled his head almost constantly.

She watched him with eyelids heavy, lips swollen. The tips of her generous breasts were tightly furled raspberry buds. He wanted to explore every inch of her creamy skin and lush curves, but the refrain in his head demanded action. *Take her, take her, take her.*

"Sorry," he muttered. "We'll go slower next time."

Before she could respond, he filled her with one firm thrust. His vision went dark. The feel of her body clasping his rigid shaft fried his brain. He was so hard his eyeballs ached. Her sex gripped him in damp, soft heat.

Slender feminine arms wrapped around his neck. Abby arched her back and canted her hips. He shuddered, gasping for breath. He was so close to coming, every nerve in his body tensed.

Abby whispered his name. "Duncan…"

Her breath was warm on his cheek.

Some primal urge, hitherto unknown, told him she belonged to him. He wanted to claim her and mark her and keep every other man away. She was *his* Abby, no one else's.

Gradually, he found a measure of control, enough to make love to her without embarrassing himself. His jaw ached from the effort and sweat dampened his brow. But he managed to reign in the beast.

Slowly, he withdrew and lazily filled her again. The rhythm was as old as time and yet new and bemusing. Had he ever wanted a woman so desperately? Had he ever connected with a woman so quickly and so intensely?

The comparisons made him uneasy, so he shoved them away, concentrating instead on nothing but the moment and Abby.

She seemed so small beneath him and infinitely fragile. Yet he knew her vulnerability was only an illusion. She was strong and resilient, and she had given him help when he needed it most.

Tenderness sneaked in, tempering his raw passion.

His breathing was ragged, his heartbeat a cacophony of drums. He took her slowly and carefully, cupping her bottom in his hands and driving deep.

Abby's cheeks were flushed, her pupils dilated. When she tried to shut him out by closing her eyes, he shook his head. "Look at me, Abby," he demanded. "Tell me what you feel."

Her blush deepened, her gaze dreamy. "You," she said. "I feel you. And there's a lot of you."

The wry commentary surprised a laugh from him. That was new, too. Humor during sex. He wasn't accustomed to the range of emotions Abby drew from him. One moment he was blind with lust, the next he wanted to cradle her in his arms and protect her from everything and everyone, even him.

Inevitably, his libido wrested control. With his heartbeat slugging in his rib cage and his chest heaving with the effort to breathe, he rested his weight on one hand and fondled her breasts. "I hope you don't really want to sleep tonight," he muttered.

Abby's smile was a mix of bashful small-town girl and newly born seductress. "Don't worry, big guy. I can keep up with you."

The end, when it came, was sheer madness. He thrust wildly, barely in control. "Abby," he groaned. "Sweet Abby…"

And then he hit the peak and lost his way.

A million hours later—or maybe it was only seconds that had passed—he regained his speech, though his tongue felt thick and his head was muzzy. "Are you okay, lass?"

His not inconsiderable weight rested completely on top of her.

Abby wriggled and freed one of her arms. "I'm good."

The prim response made him chuckle. "I suppose we should get some sleep."

"Hold that thought. I need to…well, you know…"

She was cute when she was shy. He let her escape to the bathroom. Rolling onto his back, he linked his hands behind his head and stared at the ornate plaster ceiling. Maybe he should keep her here in this hotel room for more than a single night. To hell with responsibility and expectations.

A man deserved a vacation, right?

Knowing his Puritan-work-ethic Abby, she wouldn't go for it.

When she returned, her feet made no sound at all on the carpet. She was still naked. He took that as a good sign. There were two plush bathrobes hanging on the back of the bathroom door. She could have used one. But she didn't.

In her hand, she held a washcloth.

"What's that for?" he asked, not really caring, but trying to act nonchalant. The sight of her naked body was already having a predictable effect.

Abby's smile was smug and adorable. "I'm going to clean you up, and then it's payback time."

He sat up, mildly alarmed. "That's not necessary."

"Trust me, Duncan. I've got you."

Her deliberate use of his earlier refrain told him that Abby was intent on a bit of *quid pro quo*.

When she sat on the edge of the mattress at his hip and calmly removed the condom, he quaked inwardly.

Already, his erection showed signs of new life. Then Abby took him in her hand and soaped him up, and he fell back on the bed, groaning.

Moments later, he gasped. "I think you can stop now," he said.

"Just rinsing," she said airily.

His erection was hard as stone and throbbing. "Please stop," he croaked.

Abby tossed the rag on the floor and leaned over him, bracing her hands on either side of his head. She kissed him softly. "I didn't know you were such a baby. Was I being too rough? Too hard on you?"

The prospect of his Abby being rough with him made him insane. He curled one hand behind her neck and dragged her down for a kiss. "You have a competitive streak. How did I not know that?"

She nipped his bottom lip with sharp teeth. "There's a lot you don't know. Shall I begin, or do you want to talk some more?"

He was torn between laughter and arousal. "You're scaring me," he said, only half-joking.

Abby gave him one last kiss and scooted down in the bed. "I'm only getting started."

Thirteen

Abby had never been uninhibited in her sexual relationships. Cautious by nature, she preferred to guard herself against hurt and the possibility of appearing naive or clumsy.

With Duncan, all her usual reservations vanished in the euphoria of being with a man who made her feel like a sexual goddess. The Scotsman *wanted* her. He couldn't hide it. His passionate need pushed her past her hang-ups and made her want to match his erotic expertise.

She hoped her enthusiasm would make up for anything she lacked in experience or technique.

At the moment, Duncan looked like a man being stretched on the rack. His fingers gripped folds of the sheets. His jaw clenched. She brushed her thumb over his closed eyelids. "Relax, Duncan. I won't bite... much."

Hot color swept from his throat to his hairline. His broad, hair-dusted chest heaved. "Ye're cruel, lass. Don't tease me. I'm on a hair trigger."

Since the man had enjoyed a prolonged and impressive orgasm very recently, she took his protests with a grain of salt. "Try counting sheep," she said. "Or reciting the multiplication tables. I'm in a mood to play."

Scooting down in the bed, she reclined on one elbow and studied her lover's body. His abdomen was taut and firm. She stroked the silky hair above his navel and smiled when he flinched.

His penis was both beautiful and masculine. It reared against his belly, full and thick and long. Lightly, she circled the head with her fingertip. A single drop of fluid leaked from the slit. She spread the moisture, her heart thumping as she imagined him entering her again.

Having him momentarily at her mercy was a novel experience.

Then, giving him no verbal warning at all, she went down on him, taking all of him that she could manage in her mouth and tasting his essence. A lingering bit of soap remained. But that was the least of her worries. Now that she had him, what was she supposed to do with him?

Duncan's entire body went rigid. He muttered something in Gaelic that was either a prayer or a curse. Between her lips, his erection flexed and thickened a millimeter more.

More than anything, she wanted to give him the

blissful intimacy he had shown her. Gently, she scooped his testicles into her free hand and stroked him. The effect on Duncan was electric. He tried to sit up, but she snapped out a warning. "Don't move."

He fell back onto the mattress, groaning deep in his chest. He was caught now, his vulnerability trapped in her grasp. With one hand below and the other wrapped around the base of his erection, she moved her mouth up and down, learning intimately the spots that made him shudder with pleasure.

Unfortunately, Duncan was too primed for much of her gentle torture. She could actually *feel* the urgency in him, the need to come. With one last carnal kiss, she released him. "Please tell me you have more condoms."

"Wallet," he croaked. "One more."

Abby found what she was after and fumbled to tear it open and roll the latex onto Duncan's shaft. "There," she sighed. "We're good to go."

What happened next was so fast, Duncan's movements were a blur. He dragged her to the side of the bed, bent her over and pressed her cheek to the mattress. Then he entered her slowly from behind. With this angle, he felt bigger still. Or perhaps her body was sensitive from his earlier lovemaking.

Now *she* was the one pinned and helpless. The feel of him surrounding her, dominating her, ignited her own fuse. She had been on a slow burn, never entirely sated. The way she felt at the moment, one night was never going to be enough. Could she fight for him? Was there any chance at all?

Duncan slowed his thrusts, backing her away from the precipice. She didn't want to savor. She wanted the hot flame, the blind rush. "Don't stop," she begged. He had one hand on the back of her neck. Her nape tingled.

"I'm in charge now, Abby," he said, the words guttural. "You had your chance. Now we'll do this my way."

Duncan was drunk with lust and testosterone. He wanted to pound his way to the end, but he also craved the chance to make Abby fly...to scream out his name...to know that in bed, at least, they were perfect together.

Her heart-shaped ass curved upward to a narrow waist. The line of her spine was feminine and delicate. Her reddish-blond hair made a cute wavy halo around her head.

"Give me your hands," he said.

She shot him a confused look over her shoulder. Her arms were above her head.

He clarified. "Put your hands behind your back."

Slowly, she did as he asked. Now he could manacle her wrists with one hand and steady his other hand on her rounded butt. It was a win-win for any man.

He gripped her wrists and pumped his hips. Reaching beneath her, he found that one, tiny sensitive spot and stroked it firmly. The keening sound from Abby tore through him like a shot of adrenaline. He kept up his carnal assault until he lost control and had to release her wrists. Now, with both hands caressing her sexy-as-hell butt, he groaned, picked up the pace, and shot them both over the finish line.

When it was done, he slumped on top of her, wondering what the hell had happened. He'd never gotten off on dominating a woman. Something about Abby made him want to play that game. Perhaps it was the absolute certainty that she was woman enough to meet him halfway and match his brash, demanding love play. How could anything as powerful as this be temporary, or even worse, a female game to manipulate him?

He tried to breathe, but he had forgotten how. Slowly, moving like an old man, he dragged himself and her up onto the bed and retrieved the covers. "Sleep," he mumbled. "We need sleep."

When he surfaced the next morning, it took several long minutes for the fog to clear. He and Abby had found each other twice more during the night. The memories of sex were dreamlike, but the pleasurable aches in his body were very real.

He squinted toward the window where a weak ray of sunshine peeked in around the curtains. An hour ago, barely conscious, he had stumbled to the bathroom and taken care of urgent business. Afterward, he had fallen immediately back into bed.

Now, Abby was curled into a ball with her bottom pressed to his pelvis. He stroked her hair lazily, trying to process what had happened. Yesterday had encompassed a wealth of emotional turmoil and difficult experiences. His deep gratitude for Abby's support didn't come close to explaining why he had just experienced the most amazing night of sex in his life.

She opened her eyes, shifted onto her back and looked up at him. "Hello."

He cupped her cheek and kissed her nose. "Hello,

yourself." He liked her like this, all drowsy and vulnerable.

"What time is it?"

He rolled away momentarily and glanced at the clock on the bedside table. "Ten."

Abby squeaked. "Please tell me you hung out the Do Not Disturb sign."

"I did."

"We have to check out."

"Yeah." The reluctance he heard in her voice mirrored the feelings in his gut. "What if I order room service? I'll let you have the bathroom first."

"That would be nice."

"What would you like? Eggs? Pastries?"

Her lips quirked. "At the risk of sounding unladylike, order it all. I'm starving."

"Well, you *did* work off quite a few calories last night." He said it with a straight face.

A tiny frown appeared between her perfect brows. "Are you mocking me, Mr. Stewart? How rude."

He nuzzled her neck and cupped the closest breast, closing his eyes and breathing a sigh of bliss. "No mocking, lass. Only a reminder." He took her chin and turned her to meet his lips. "I'm verra grateful for all the aerobic activity. You keep a man on his toes, wicked girl."

Abby smirked and kissed him warmly. "You're not so bad yourself."

When he tried to slide his hand between her warm thighs, she batted it away. "No time for that. You promised me food."

With a long-suffering sigh, he stood up and stretched. "If you insist."

For the second time, he availed himself of the facilities in the sitting room. Grabbing jeans and a navy knit Henley, he made short work of cleaning up and getting dressed. Fortunately, he was close enough to the front door to hear when the bellman delivered the meal.

Abby appeared just as Duncan was tipping the hotel employee. Like Duncan, she had opted for jeans and a knit shirt. Hers was pink. A pale pink that clung to her breasts and made him want to say to hell with the meal and take her straight back to bed.

He had ordered an obscene amount of food. Between them, they devoured it all.

His breakfast guest stared at the empty tray as she drank her second cup of coffee. "Wow. I think I'm embarrassed."

"I like a woman with a hearty appetite...for everything."

Now her cheeks were pinker than her shirt. "The sun is up. We shouldn't be thinking about sex."

"Well, you're out of luck, because I'm always thinking about sex when I'm around you."

"Really?"

It occurred to him that she thought he was kidding. He leaned over, put a hand behind her head and pulled her close enough to give her a hungry kiss. "Really, Abby."

When he released her, they were both breathing hard. "Stay at the house with me this week," he said impulsively.

Abby bit her lip. "I don't think that's a good idea. I *will* help you every day. I promised you I would. But I'll go home in the evenings."

He scowled, feeling remarkably surly for a man who had spent the better part of the night in nirvana. "Why?"

She shrugged, her expression hard to read. "I'd rather make the break now. You're leaving soon. This is hard enough already, because I care about you. Not to mention the fact that you're going to have people in and out of the house this week. I can't risk the gossip, Duncan. When you're nothing but a memory, I still have to live and work here. My job and my reputation are important to me."

His temper skyrocketed. "So this is it?"

"What do you want from me?"

Only the pain in her eyes kept him from yelling at her. He tempered his response with difficulty. "Maybe you could give me a chance to figure a few things out."

"To what end? I live here. You live there. We've had great sex, and that's about the only thing we have in common. I don't want to talk about this anymore. Take me back to Candlewick, please."

The hour-long trip home was awkward at first, neither of them speaking at all. Eventually, he decided he was too tired to stay mad. Abby's rules made sense, even if he didn't like them.

He reached across the space separating them and took her hand. "We'll handle this however you think is best. And I won't hold you to your promise to help."

She squeezed his fingers. "You need me for a few days. You can't simply let a company come in and take it all. I know you think you don't want anything, but there might be valuables we need to find...if not for you personally, then perhaps for Brody's kids. Or yours."

"I don't plan on having kids," he said, putting both hands on the wheel.

"Oh?"

"Too much responsibility. And it's not fair to the kids when the parents break up."

"You speak from experience."

"Yeah. I told you before that I don't like secrets. That was the problem with my parents. They thought they were protecting Brody and me by shielding us from the problems they were having. They kept up appearances…never argued and yelled in front of us. I suppose on the surface that seemed like the civilized thing to do."

"But it wasn't?"

"Hell, no. Brody and I were completely blindsided when they split up. It tore the ground from beneath our feet. We felt stupid and betrayed. I don't know what we would have done without Granny and Grandda to look after us in the midst of all the nastiness when everything imploded."

"Not all marriages end."

"But a lot of them do. So I'd just as soon not take the chance." He took a deep breath, his hands white-knuckled on the steering wheel. "Can we change the subject, please?"

"Of course."

Several miles passed in silence before Abby spoke again. "Tell me about working for your brother," she said. "Do you enjoy it?"

"I do." In fact, he missed being at his desk with the view of the loch more than he realized he would.

"And are water and boats your passion like they are for Brody?"

Duncan chuckled. "Not entirely. I love Skye. 'Tis a beautiful place to grow up. But for me, it's the mountains that call. A couple of years ago, I began climbing the Munros in Scotland. I've managed twenty-three so far."

"Munros? I don't know what that means."

"In Scotland, it's the term we use for any summit that's over three thousand feet. There are almost three hundred in all. So I've quite a way to go. When I thought I'd be living here with Granny, I had explored the idea of hiking in the Blue Ridge. I fell in love with your mountains when Brody and I spent summers here as kids."

"We do have some spectacular ones. Very different from Scotland, I'd say."

"Indeed. Ours are mostly bare and windswept. Here, you have peaks twice as tall and very hard to get to."

"Well," Abby said with a cheerfulness that was clearly forced, "maybe you'll find time to take at least one hike before you leave."

After that, they were both silent again. The easy intimacy they had shared during the night didn't hold up in the light of day. Plus, Abby seemed determined to remind him he was leaving.

When they arrived in the outskirts of Candlewick, Duncan steered the car up the mountain. He wasn't about to give Abby an opportunity to ask if he would drop her off at her house.

His grandparents' home already looked sad and

abandoned. It made no sense, really. Nothing had changed except for the inhabitants.

Duncan unloaded their bags. Someone had left two flower arrangements on the front porch. While he read the sympathy cards, Abby kept her distance. After last night, the walls she was trying to erect between them pissed him off, even though he didn't really know what he wanted from her. Was he afraid that she was angling for marriage and children?

Inside, he stared at her. "Lunch?"

"I won't need anything until dinner," she said, her gaze not meeting his. "I think I'll get started on that first bedroom."

"Fine. Suit yourself."

"What will you do?"

"I suppose I'll tackle the office. Granny tried cleaning it out when Brody and Cate were here with her, but it was too much. She made me promise to do it with her."

Abby came to him then and put her arms around his waist, resting her cheek on his chest. "I'm sorry she's gone, Duncan."

He held her tightly. "Aye. She was a hell of a woman. I hope she and Grandda can't see what I'm about to do."

"You have to decide what you think is best for you and your family. That's all anyone can ask."

She took a step back, and he was forced to release her. "I found trash bags in the kitchen yesterday," she said. "I'll use white ones for things we're donating and the black ones for stuff that needs to be thrown out. Is that okay with you?"

Suddenly, the whole damn situation suffocated

him. His grandparents' business empire. Abby's expectations of him, both personally and as a lawyer. His own ambivalence about everything. "Do what you want," he said curtly. "I don't really care."

When she turned on her heel and walked away from him, he wanted to drag her back and apologize. But maybe it was better this way. If she thought he was a jerk, she wouldn't want him to hang around... right?

Though his heart wasn't in it, he went to his grandfather's office and began the daunting task of separating wheat from chaff. The detritus of decades-filled drawers and covered tabletops. There were hundreds of maps and architectural drawings. He felt comfortable pitching all that because the important ones could be found downtown at Stewart Properties headquarters.

It was galling to admit that Abby had been right. Almost immediately, he had to begin filling a box with small items that were too valuable or too historically significant to pitch. Maybe a local museum would like to have the knickknacks and programs from the 1950s and 1960s. All of it was interesting, but if Duncan began reading each little pamphlet and check and receipt, he'd be here until the end of time.

A second, larger box was required for the cloth-bound notebooks. His grandparents had both kept journals, particularly from the years when they struggled to establish their business. In the prosperity of post–World War II, Isobel and Geoffrey's foresight in predicting the upcoming tourist boom had given them an edge in the empire they began so modestly.

One glance at a few of the entries was enough to

tell Duncan that his brother and sister-in-law would want to see these. Once he had them all together, he could seal the box and ship it to Scotland. It would cost a fortune, but it would be worth it.

After a couple of hours, be began to feel a sense of accomplishment. He worked quickly but methodically, ignoring the urge to go down the hall and see how Abby was faring.

If she wanted distance between them, he would try to comply, even if it killed him. She was right about one thing. It would be damned easy to fall in love. And there was nothing for her in Scotland. Her career was right here in Candlewick. Reading between the lines, Duncan felt certain that her boss planned for Abby to take over one day. Why else would the man have devoted to much time and attention to her schooling?

Duncan tucked the last two journals in the box but left the top open in case he found more. As he bent to set the heavy carton on the floor in the corner, he spotted the edge of something sticking out from behind the large oak filing cabinet.

It was a large, heavy vellum envelope. His grandfather's scrawling handwriting was immediately recognizable. Clearly, the envelope had never been opened. On the front were the words *My Dearest Isobel*. The salutation was innocuous enough, but for some reason, dread slithered through Duncan's veins. What could his grandfather have written that was only now coming to light over a year after the old man's death?

Fourteen

Abby straightened, yawned and stretched to get the kinks out of her back. She had carried multiple arm-loads of clothing from the closet to the bed so she could go through the pockets. Even so, she'd done a lot of bending and lifting. Her nose itched, probably from the scent of all the mothballs. Isobel had been determined that no feckless moth would ever get a crack at her and Geoffrey's winter wardrobes.

In two hours, Abby had made a huge dent in clean-ing out this particular guest room. The closet was now empty, as were all the drawers in the furniture and in the bathroom. All that was left was to strip the bed.

Sadly, Duncan had been right about the fact that most things would end up in the rubbish bin. Much of the clothing was too dated to donate but not old enough to be of interest to a museum. Hence the fact that Abby now had a dozen huge trash bags ready to go to a Dumpster when the time was right.

When it came to finding valuable things to keep, so far she had collected seven sticks of spearmint chewing gum, four orphaned buttons, and a *Carter for President* button. The only possible standout in her collection was a small gold tie tack in the shape of a fleur-de-lis.

She put the odds and ends on the bedside table and went into the bathroom to splash her face with cold water. Her lack of sleep the night before was beginning to catch up with her. In the mirror, her eyes were bright. Despite the hard work, she was happy to be here with Duncan.

Making a face at her reflection, she sighed. "Stupid woman. You should run. This isn't going to end well for you."

Mirror Abby didn't seem any more sensible than her flesh-and-blood twin. She returned to the bedroom and found Duncan standing in the doorway. When she smiled at him, he didn't seem to notice. His face was dead white and his hands clenched an envelope.

Alarmed by his pallor and his demeanor, she went to him immediately. "What is it? What's wrong?"

The muscles in his throat worked as he swallowed. "I found a note. From my grandfather. To my grandmother. One she apparently never saw. It's dated ten days before he died."

"Oh, Duncan. How sad. I'm sorry. But they're together now, so if you think about it, the note isn't really that important, is it?" She was trying to cheer him up, but it wasn't working.

"It's bad, Abby."

Her stomach clenched. "Bad how?" Geoffrey hadn't committed suicide. She knew that. Such a thing would have been impossible to hide in a small town. From what she remembered, the old man died of a stroke.

Duncan hadn't moved from his position in the doorway. His eyes were pools of misery and shock. "Read it," he said gruffly. "I don't know what to do."

Now she was frightened. What could possibly be so terrible? Duncan's grandfather had been married to his grandmother forever. This couldn't be one of those scenarios where he had a secret family. No other possibility came to mind. Unless he had been unfaithful and wanted to clear his conscience. Surely it wasn't that.

With trembling fingers, she took the envelope and extracted the single sheet of eight-and-a-half-by-eleven onionskin paper. Geoffrey Stewart had typed his note, presumably on the old Royal manual machine Abby had seen in the office. She took a breath and started reading…

My dearest Isobel—
If you are reading this, I'm guessing that I have passed on and you are left to unravel the mess I have made of things. My only excuse is that I believe I have been experiencing the onset of dementia. Much of what I am about to tell you refers to events of which I have no real memory. I suppose that sounds like the worst of excuses, but it is true.

Some weeks ago, a gentleman came to me

with an investment proposal. He was very persuasive, and apparently I agreed to let him make a purchase on my behalf. I do not even recall the nature of the business proposition, but I took five million dollars out of our account and gave it to him.

All the money is gone, Isobel. All of it. I am an old fool, and I should have handed over the reins of the company long ago. The auditors were here only last week, so it will be a year at least before anyone finds out what I have done. I did not mortgage our business, thank the good Lord, but I have made such terrible inroads into our liquid assets that it will be difficult to recover.

My hope is that I will be able to somehow replace the money. If that is the case, you will never have to know, and I will destroy this note. I am frightened and distraught. You put your faith in me, and I have betrayed you terribly.

I find that my grasp on things is tenuous some days. I want to tell you the truth. I want you to know that my mind wanders. I am so ashamed, and I find it difficult to speak of these things. A man is supposed to care for the ones he loves. How can I do that when I don't always remember how to find our home at the end of a long day?

In case there is the slightest chance that our funds might somehow be recovered, I am enclosing the business card I found in my suit pocket. The man's name is Howard Lander...

Abby gasped and dropped the letter, her hands numb. *No. Please, God, no.*

Duncan misread her shock. "I told you it was bad. Five million dollars, Abby. I won't even be able to sell the company now. With the assets decimated, people may lose their jobs. This was going to come to light soon enough. I don't know how to tell Brody. And what about the employees? How do I explain that my grandfather was senile?"

He shouted the last question. His face was stark white.

Abby could barely speak. "We'll figure something out, Duncan. You could sell a few of the cabins. Restructure. My boss will help you, I'm sure."

Duncan's lips thinned and his scowl sent ice down Abby's spine. "Or I could hunt down this Howard Lander fellow and make him wish he had never been born."

Already Abby was wishing the very same thing. She swallowed hard. "Give yourself a moment to breathe. It may not be as bad as you think."

"I appreciate your attempt to comfort me, Abby, but all the positive thinking in the world isn't going to make five million dollars magically appear."

His cynical response crushed her. First his grandmother's unexpected death, and now this. She had to tell him the truth, but the words stuck in her throat. She knew exactly who Howard Lander was and where to find him. If she told Duncan that Howard was her father, Duncan would eye her with contempt and distrust. He would never believe she'd had nothing to do with the scheme to defraud his grandparents. He would think she had kept this horrific secret. But she hadn't. It wasn't true. She was as shocked as he was.

Nausea flooded her stomach. "Would you mind taking me home, Duncan? I think I've done all I can for one day. I'm really tired, and I just remembered an appointment I shouldn't miss."

A frown appeared between his brows. "You're not staying?"

"I'll come back in the morning."

He reached for her hand. "I'm sorry if I've upset you. Please don't go, Abby."

His sweet, weary smile tore the heart out of her chest. Her terrible secret choked her. She wanted to console and comfort him, and yet she was the last person who should be with him at this moment. Now it was far too late to wish she had told him all about her father and his failings. Her silence on the subject would condemn her when the truth came out. Before that happened, she had to at least try to find a solution.

She allowed herself the luxury of leaning into him for one blissful second and then another. At last, she forced herself to step away. "It's not you. It's me. You haven't done anything wrong. Not at all. But I do need to go home for a bit. Please. Or let me take your grandmother's old car."

He shuddered. "Not that. It's a piece of junk. I'll take you down the mountain if that's what you want."

It wasn't what she wanted. But she had no choice.

Twenty minutes later, they were back in the car. Abby had her suitcase and her shattered dreams. Once the truth came to light, Duncan would look at her with disgust and scorn.

More important than her own sorrow was Duncan's terrible situation. Abby had to do something—anything—to undo the damage that had been done. To right the wrongs.

She and Duncan didn't speak during the drive down the mountain. Eventually, an icy calm replaced her near hysteria. She had faced difficult situations before. This was no different.

Liar. Her conscience screamed condemnation. It didn't matter how very hard she tried not to be her father's daughter. His blood ran in her veins, and his transgressions were written in indelible ink on her ledger sheet. How would she ever make it up to Duncan?

At her house, he kept the engine running. "Thank you, Abby," he said.

His gratitude was a slap in the face under the circumstances. She managed a small smile. "Are you thanking me for sex?"

"It's a blanket thank-you," he said, leaning over to kiss her forehead. "I couldn't have survived all this without you."

The protective ice around her heart began to melt, allowing the gargantuan pain to return. "I wanted to be with you, Duncan. I still do."

"I'll text you in the morning. Does that work?"

She searched his face, looking for some sign that the intimacies they had shared were more than commonplace for him. "Will you be okay tonight?" *Alone...*

He nodded slowly. "I'll have an early night."

"Don't brood about the money."

"That's like telling the sun not to come up. Don't worry about that, Abby. It's not your problem."

She fled the car and escaped into her house, barely closing the door behind her before she collapsed onto her bed. For half an hour, she sobbed. Already she missed Duncan with a dreadful ache that was like a black hole sucking her into oblivion...

When she was too empty for tears anymore, she lay there and tried to breathe. Her chest hurt. Her head hurt. Her stomach hurt. But she didn't have the luxury of wallowing in her grief.

Feeling light-headed and sick, she got to her feet and went into the bathroom to wash her face. Then, before she could lose her nerve, she grabbed her car keys and walked out of the house.

Her father lived on the fringes of Candlewick in a trailer park that had seen better days. The police regularly made meth busts in the area. Surprisingly, her father had never dabbled in drugs. He seemed quite happy with his whisky and his cigarettes.

She parked in front of his rusted mobile home and got out. This was the first time in more than six years that she had actually sought him out and not the other way around. When she pressed the peeling, discolored buzzer, she had to battle the urge to run.

Howard Lander flung open his door and stared at her, his mouth slack with shock. "My baby. Abby. I'm so glad to see you."

When he went to hug her, she held him at bay with a hand to his chest. "Save it, old man. This is business." She pushed past him into the tiny living room and began to have doubts. Her father lived in near poverty. His furniture was made up of mismatched thrift store finds.

Could the note Duncan found have been no more than the ramblings of a very sick man? *Please, God, let it be so.*

She couldn't bring herself to sit down, so she stood. Her father sprawled in his recliner and hit the mute button on the TV. "To what do I owe the pleasure?" he asked, grimacing.

"What did you do with Geoffrey Stewart's money?"

Even then, she hoped her father would look blank.

Unfortunately, his response left no room for misinterpretation. His puffy face turned red. Fear filled his eyes. His expression was equal parts haunted and terrified. "I don't know what you're talking about."

She wrapped her arms around her waist to keep from shattering into pieces. "I know about the five million dollars. I want it back."

Howard switched from guilty fear to bluster. "Do I look like a man who has five million?"

"Maybe you're hiding it so no one will be onto you. But I know. Duncan knows, too. Geoffrey Stewart left a note. And he admitted everything. Your business card was in the envelope. How could you, Daddy?"

Her voice broke on the last word. How many times could a man disappoint his child before the relationship was irrevocably destroyed?

Howard switched to attack mode. It was a familiar pattern whenever life backed him into a corner. "The old coot had more money than he could ever spend in a lifetime. I didn't do nothin' wrong. He gave it to me of his own free will."

"The man had dementia," Abby yelled. "You took advantage of him."

"It's not like he was gonna miss the money." Howard sulked.

"I want it back. Where is it?"

"It's gone."

"Gone where?"

"I had a run of bad luck at the craps tables in Biloxi. I thought I could double the cash. Make five mil for myself and pay the old boy back. But it didn't go my way."

Abby thought for a moment she was going to be physically ill. "We have to make this right," she said desperately.

Howard shook his head. "Are you out of your mind? We could sell this trailer and your house, and that wouldn't even be a drop in the bucket. The cash is gone. End of story. Those Stewarts are richer than God. This is a blip on their radar. You worry too much about nothing, girl."

Anger seared through her veins. "And what if Duncan Stewart sends you to prison? What then?"

Her father gaped at her. "You wouldn't let that happen. I know you, Abby. You're my kid. I'm the only thing you've got."

She backed away from him, sick and heartbroken. Her naïveté was astounding. She had worried that being in a relationship with Duncan was dangerous. That the temporary affair might mean losing her job, her reputation. Even worse, her heart.

But all along, her blood, her family sins, were the real ticking bomb. Like Duncan, she had been blindsided by a secret. And like Duncan, she felt stupid and betrayed.

And all because she wanted so badly to have a parent, any parent, to love her.

"You're not anything to me," she said dully. "Don't ever come near me again. As of Monday, I'll have a restraining order in place. You no longer have the right to call yourself my father. How does it feel to know you gambled that away, too?"

She jerked open the door and stumbled outside. Curious neighbors watched her climb into her car. Abby ignored them. With trembling hands, she sent Lara a text. Can you meet me at my house? It's an emergency. The bank had closed fifteen minutes ago. She was counting on the fact that her friend would be free.

When Abby pulled into her own driveway, Lara was already sitting on her porch. Abby walked up the steps and into Lara's arms. This time, the tears were far beyond her control. She lost it completely.

Lara hustled her inside and into the kitchen. Abby sank into a chair and buried her face in her arms. Her friend didn't say a word. Instead, she put the kettle on to boil and found Abby's favorite tea bags.

"Here," Lara said some time later. "Drink this."

"I don't think I can." Abby choked out the words. Her stomach heaved, but after a few cautious sips, the scent and the taste of the familiar drink helped calm her. In the silence of the kitchen, she could hear a clock ticking. Her life was in ruins, but the world went on.

Lara wet a paper towel and handed it across the

table. "Wipe your face and take a breath. Then tell me everything."

The whole sordid tale came tumbling out. Abby glossed over the trip to Asheville after the funeral, but Lara read between the lines. When Abby arrived at the part about the note and the money and her father's involvement, Lara got quiet and her frown deepened.

Abby clenched her hands on the table. "So that's it. Do you think I could get a loan at the bank? It might take me a lifetime to pay the money back, but I have to do something."

Lara grimaced. "Here's the thing, kid. You have excellent credit. But no one in his or her right mind is going to loan you five million dollars. Speaking as a banking professional, I'm telling you that's not going to happen. I'm sorry."

"Oh." Abby absorbed the blow. "How much *could* I borrow?"

The other woman reached across the table and took Abby's hands in hers. "Look at me, love. It's your father's debt. Not yours."

"You don't understand," Abby muttered.

"I understand more than you think. That asshole has been a millstone around your neck for most of your life. But he's not *you*, Abby. Everyone in this town knows who you are. They see your honor. Your integrity. As much as this hurts, you're going to have to find a way to let it go. A terrible wrong was perpetrated on the Stewart family. But they're not destitute. They'll recover."

"I have to tell Duncan the truth."

"Of course you do. And sooner rather than later. But if the Scotsman is half the man you think he is, he'll accept the fact that you aren't responsible for your father's way of life."

"I'm scared."

Lara came around the table and put her arms around Abby. "I would be, too, if I were in your shoes. But the truth is always best. Call your Duncan and tell him everything."

Abby wiped her face with her hands, unable to entirely stem the tears that came and went. Her throat closed up. Regrets strangled her. "I know we didn't have much of a chance. Everything was temporary from day one. He was going to leave. But I didn't want it to end like this."

"No matter what happens, I'm here for you, Abby. You're my best friend in the whole world. You don't have to do this alone."

The other woman's affection threatened Abby's hard-won composure. She stood up and hugged her friend. "I'm okay now. I'll keep you posted."

Lara cocked her head and stared. "You sure?"

Abby nodded, her lips numb and her heart aching. "I'll have an early night. Things always look better in the morning. Isn't that what they say?"

"The good news is they couldn't look much worse."

"Go home," Abby said, actually managing a genuine smile. "With friends like you, who needs enemies?"

When Lara was gone, Abby took out her phone and sent a text. What time do you want to start in the morning?

Duncan's reply was immediate. Let's wait until Wednesday. I have several things to deal with in the morning.

Her heart sank. Was he putting her off, or was he really busy? She tapped out another message. Would you like to come to my house for an early dinner tomorrow night? We need to talk about a few things.

This time his response soothed her nerves. I'd like that. What time?

Five thirty?

I'll be there.

She hesitated but took the risk. I miss you...

I miss you, too, lass.

Fifteen

Duncan spent a largely sleepless night searching for answers. He hadn't called Brody yet. It seemed pointless to upset the rest of the family until Duncan had some answers and a plan for a way forward.

In between worrying about his grandparents' business and legacy, he thought about Abby. His bed had never seemed emptier than it did right now. Twenty-four hours ago, he and his curvy playmate had been burning up the sheets. One reason he had waved her off for tomorrow was that he wanted to get a handle on his feelings.

When he was with her, everything seemed right. Without asking, she had inserted herself into his tragedy and cared for him at a time when he was most vulnerable and alone. The past few days would have been virtually unbearable had he not had Abby at his side.

But something bothered him still. Her refusal to talk about her father for one thing. It seemed an odd omission. And when Duncan had showed Abby the letter from Howard Lander, she went white, her expression beyond distraught. Was she really that empathetic, or was there something she wasn't telling him?

Now, he lay awake…on his back…staring up at the ceiling. Wishing he could hold her and touch her and kiss her and bury himself in her welcoming warmth. Abby had told him she didn't want a broken heart. Is that what was happening? Were the two of them falling in love? Against all odds, had Duncan come to America and found a missing piece of himself?

He doubted his own instincts. He'd been drowning in family drama for days now. Everything was magnified. The good. The bad. Maybe sweet Abby was an attractive life raft. A distraction.

After 2:00 a.m., he managed to sleep for an hour at a time. But at sunup, he was out of bed and in the shower, determined to get his life back on track. Tonight, he looked forward to spending time with Abby. The prospect was the dangling carrot that would propel him through the day.

When his grandparents' bank opened at nine, Duncan was on the doorstep. Five minutes later— despite the fact that he didn't have an appointment— he was sitting in the bank president's office.

The man seemed curious, but welcoming. "How can I help you, Mr. Stewart?"

Duncan drummed his fingers on the leather-covered chair arms. "Just before he died, my grandfather made an extremely large withdrawal from one of his accounts. Were you aware of that?"

The man nodded. "I remember. An amount like that is hard to forget."

"And you didn't try to stop him?"

A frown appeared on the dignified president's face. "We are not in the business of keeping customers *away* from their money, Mr. Stewart. Your grandfather filled out the appropriate paperwork, and he made the transfer to a bank in a nearby town. I assumed he was opening another account. Not my business to interfere."

Duncan ground his teeth. "Were you also aware that my grandfather was experiencing signs of dementia?"

The man paled. "I was not. Your grandfather was a well-respected businessman. It would never have occurred to me to interfere with his transaction."

"Even for his own good?"

"We're not social workers, Mr. Stewart. We're bankers. Did others know about this?"

"Unfortunately, no. Or if my grandmother did, she never admitted it to any of us."

"Then how are you making this assumption?"

"It's not an assumption. It's fact." Duncan reached into his coat pocket and extracted the crumpled letter. "Take a look."

Duncan saw the man's face change as he absorbed the contents of the letter. His shock and dismay were much the same as Abby's had been. "I'm very sorry," he said. "This is dreadful."

"Aye. Have you heard of this fellow?"

"Oh, yes…unfortunately. He's lived in Candlewick for many years. And you know his daughter, I'm sure?"

"His daughter?" Duncan's stomach clenched the moment before the words were spoken aloud.

The bank president nodded. "Abby Hartmann. Poor girl has had to deal with her father's transgressions her entire life. He's a grifter and a con man. I'll admit, though, this is the first time I've ever known him to attempt something on this scale."

Duncan had gone blind and deaf. The other man was still talking, but none of it made sense. Outside the bay window, a storm lashed the streets, ushering in the first serious cold front of autumn. Colorful leaves fell like rain. Duncan studied a rivulet on the glass and watched it slide from top to bottom.

The only two words echoing in his head were the most unbelievable. *Abby Hartmann.*

The feeling of shock and betrayal was absolute. Suddenly, every word she had ever spoken to him was suspect, his worst fears realized. He'd been worried about her attempt to sell Stewart Properties. That seemed laughable now. He had told her more than once how much he hated lies, and all the while she had been as duplicitous as a woman could be.

He lurched to his feet. "Thank you for your time," he muttered. The gaping hole in his chest made it hard to breathe.

"If you decide to pursue legal action, I'll cooperate in any way I can. I am very sorry, Mr. Stewart. Sorrier than you know."

With a curt nod, Duncan managed to find the door and escape. Outside, he hovered on the stoop and watched the driving sheets of rain. He was cold to the bone, but he stepped out into the deluge anyway.

There was only one destination left. And he knew the way.

Abby hummed now and again as she diced and chopped vegetables for the soup she was making. Morning had brought a modicum of peace. Every family had skeletons in its closets. Surely Duncan would understand that her father was not under her control. No matter how hard she tried, she couldn't keep her blood relation from wreaking havoc.

Even so, she dreaded the moment of truth. Having to confess her connection to the man who had robbed the Stewarts was going to stick in her throat.

Pride was partly to blame, but it was more than that. She ached for the upheaval in Duncan's life. Izzy's death was shockingly sudden yet inevitable. But Howard Lander's perfidy was the equivalent of the sports term *piling on*.

Duncan was already having a hell of a month. Now, he had even more to bear. The weight of his responsibilities to Stewart Properties and to his family must be daunting.

When her doorbell rang, she turned the soup pot on low and wiped her hands on a towel. As she approached the front door, she saw the outline of a man's head through the small fan-shaped piece of glass.

Her heart beat faster.

She yanked open the door. "Duncan. Good grief. You're soaked. What are you doing here? Let me get you some towels."

He didn't say a word, but he waited obediently

until she returned with a handful of her thickest terry cloth. In another situation, she might have helped dry him off, but something about his body language warned her not to touch.

When he was no longer dripping, they moved to the living room. Abby switched on the gas logs and sat down on the sofa. Duncan remained standing, his big frame rigid. His expression was impossible to read.

"The soup won't be ready for a few hours," she said. "but if you're hungry for lunch, I make a mean grilled cheese."

Her attempt at humor fell flat. Duncan's face was stark and pale. His dark eyes glittered with strong emotion.

He jammed his hands in his pockets and paced. "Tell me this, Abby. Were you in on it? Was all of this a grand scheme to devalue the company so that you or someone else could waltz in and snap it up for a song?"

If he had slapped her, the shock couldn't have been any greater. "You don't mean that…surely."

His scowl frightened her. "Look at it from where I'm standing. You had an inside track with my grandparents' lawyer from the beginning. No sooner did I move into my grandmother's house, than there you were, metaphorically holding my hand, making yourself indispensable. You even admitted you thought I should sell everything. How convenient for you and your father that I wanted to go back to Scotland."

Tears clogged her throat, even as her heart shredded. "*You* were the one who asked me out, Duncan. Are you forgetting that? I told you it wasn't a good idea. Now that's coming back to bite me. But I never did anything to harm you or your family. I wouldn't. I couldn't."

"Five million dollars." He looked around her modest house. "Where is it now, Abby? Where's the money? Tucked away in a Swiss bank account somewhere? Waiting for me to leave North Carolina so you can swoop in and take over everything my grandparents worked for all their lives?"

How could a man who had made love to her so tenderly stare at her with such visible disgust?

Her chin wobbled. "It's gone. I went to see my father yesterday afternoon. It's gone. He gambled it all away."

Duncan's gaze narrowed. "You lied to me, Abby, and so damned convincingly. You stood in my house and read the letter I handed you and yet you never bothered to mention that you knew the charlatan my grandda was describing. Howard Lander. Your father. Why don't you have the same last name he does? Is there a husband waiting in the wings? Is he in on this, too?"

She knew Duncan was hurt. She knew he was lashing out in his pain. But knowing didn't make the insults any easier to bear. "I legally changed my name five years ago, because I was ashamed Howard Lander was my father."

"A convenient answer."

"It's the truth."

Duncan shook his head slowly. His face was an open book for once. Disillusionment. Pain. Deep regret. Gut-level sorrow. "You were good, Abby. I have to hand it to you. I suppose it helps when your father is a con man. I actually considered the possibility that I might be falling in love with you. Ridiculous, isn't it?" He paled further. "That's why you didn't want me to meet him the day I was here with you and you were picking out dresses. You were so upset. I thought he had done something to hurt you. But it was far more sinister than that. You didn't want to risk me finding out about the money."

"I didn't *know* about the money," she shouted, tears streaming down her face. "When you showed me that letter yesterday, I wanted to die."

"And yet you didn't say a word." He threw the accusation at her without remorse, his tone flat and cold.

Silence reverberated in her little house. She scrambled for a way to make him listen.

"I was in shock. It stunned me. But that's why I invited you to dinner tonight. I was planning to tell you everything, every last wretched detail. You have to believe me."

His expression never changed. No matter what she said or did, Duncan was going to think the worst of her.

It was a hell of a moment to realize that she loved him, body and soul.

She took three steps in his direction. If she could touch him, they might be able to break through this agonizing impasse. When she laid a hand, palm flat, on his chest, he didn't flinch. His icy gaze was painful, but she bore it bravely.

"Think, Duncan," she said. "Think of what we had Monday night. That was special. You felt it, too. I gave you everything. I held nothing back. Tell me you know how much I care about you."

Beneath her fingertips, his heart slugged in his chest. He was living and breathing, his skin hot to the touch, even through his crisp dress shirt.

But the ice that encased him never cracked.

If he had been hotly furious, she might have reached him. Instead, the man she had come to know so intimately was locked away somewhere he couldn't be reached.

With two fingers, he lifted her arm away from his chest and dropped it.

"Too little, too late, lass. I'll clean up this mess. Somehow. And if I find solid evidence that you conspired with your father to defraud my family, I won't have the slightest compunction about putting you behind bars right alongside him."

The remainder of Tuesday was a blur for Duncan. He left Abby's house and went straight to his grandparents' empty mansion on the mountaintop, because it was the only place he had to go.

He'd forgotten that the minister had promised to come by with a potluck lunch. The containers were stacked neatly on the porch. With a guilty grimace, Duncan carried them inside and called the pastor to apologize and say thank you. The man's genuine concern bolstered Duncan in spite of the hellish day he was having.

The food smelled amazing, but Duncan had no appetite. He roamed the house moodily, feeling angry and off-kilter and so much more.

The rooms mocked him. He had seen Abby in almost all of them. Her presence was everywhere. Her scent. Her ghost. How could he have been so wrong about her?

Already, remorse flooded his gut. He had been cruel, harsh. What if he were wrong? The facts seemed crystal clear. Then again, his world was in such turmoil, he scarcely knew down from up. It was not hyperbole to say that Abby had been his salvation in recent days. Could her kindness be motivated by a mixture of greed and guilt? Or was she genuinely innocent? Was she speaking the truth when she said she didn't know what her father had done?

He wanted that to be true. God how he wanted that to be true. But his own parents had fooled him completely once upon a time with convincing lies. How could anyone ever know for sure what was in the heart of another person?

He contemplated going to a hotel, but that required more energy than he possessed at the moment. Sometime around six, he dug out a bottle of his grandfather's best scotch and opened it. If he was going to wallow in his own misfortune, he needed company. Right now, the whisky was the best he could do.

By the time the sun rose again, he was no closer to a solution for his problems, but he had a hell of a headache.

When the doorbell rang midmorning, his heart lurched. *Abby...*

He strode down the hallway, yanked open the door, and felt his heart fall to his feet. The woman standing on his porch was a stranger.

Before he could speak, she poked him in the chest with a sharp finger. "What did you do to her, damn it?"

The blonde with the runway body and the street-fighter attitude backed him into the house.

"Could you please not shout?" He put his hand on the top of his head and tried not to throw up.

The woman slammed the door...with her on the inside now. "I'll ask you again. What did you do to my friend?"

"Have we met?"

"Don't play coy with me, Duncan Stewart. I'm talking about Abby. What did you do to her? She's not answering her phone. Her car isn't in her garage, and she's not at work."

He cherry-picked the questions. "She took some time off. I'm sure she's fine." Even as he spouted the lie, all he could think about was the way she looked when he walked out of her house. Devastated. Defenseless. Shattered.

"Where's your kitchen?" the blonde asked, her voice curt.

Duncan pointed. "Through there."

She took his arm and force-marched him down the hall. In the cheery breakfast nook, she shoved him into a chair and turned to the counter to fill his coffee maker.

Duncan began to wonder if this was some kind of bizarre nightmare. "Who are you? What are you doing in my house?" he asked. "And do you have any acetaminophen?"

The blonde scowled. "My name is Lara Finch. I'm here to sober you up, because I need your help. I'm worried about my best friend." She reached in her purse and tossed a plastic bottle in his direction.

At this point, it seemed easier to go along with

the crazy woman. Duncan swallowed two capsules. Without water. And waited for the coffee. When the blonde handed him a steaming cup several minutes later, he almost wept.

She poured herself a mug as well and took a seat across the table from him. "When was the last time you saw her? Last night?"

He shook his head. "No." He glanced at his watch. "It's been a long time. Almost twenty-four hours."

Lara frowned. "She told me she was fixing dinner for you last night."

"Well, she didn't. I was here. Alone."

The blonde shook her head as if clearing bad information. "Okay. Let's start again. What did you do to her?"

Duncan sighed, wondering how long it would be before his head stopped pounding. "Abby and I had words yesterday morning. At her house. I left. That's it."

"You were at the bank yesterday, weren't you?"

"I'm not sure my whereabouts are any of your business."

Lara ignored him. "The bank president told you that Abby Hartmann is Howard Lander's daughter. So you put two and two together and came up with five."

"What do you know about all this?"

"She came to me Monday afternoon. She was distraught."

"Because she knew the ax was about to fall."

"Oh. My. God. Listen to yourself. *You* don't even believe what you're saying...do you?"

He stared at his coffee. "No." Suddenly, his heart jerked. "Why are you worried about her?"

"She's disappeared."

His heart stopped. "Then we have to find her." Now, in the light of day and with a few hours' sleep under his belt, the truth came to him. He was a fool, plain and simple. It didn't matter if Abby had lied or not. He wanted her. He needed her. It was as simple as that.

"We're wasting time," he said. "I'll be ready in five minutes. You're familiar with Candlewick and the surrounding area. Start making a list of any conceivable places she might have gone."

When he returned in less time than he had promised, Lara stood and crooked a finger. "Give me your keys."

"Oh, hell no."

She grinned. "Well, it was worth a try. Come on, Mr. Tall, Dark and Gorgeous. We'll take my car, then, 'cause I know all the back roads. Let's go find our Abby."

Sixteen

Duncan hated being a passenger. But he would have done anything to find Abby, even if it meant tolerating the kamikaze driving of her best friend.

Not only did Lara have a death wish on the narrow two-lane roads, she relished the chance to berate him. "You know Abby is pure gold."

"Yes." He opened his mouth to defend himself, but no words came out. He'd made the biggest mistake of his adult life and that was saying something, because he pulled some boneheaded stunts in his time. "I was upset. I felt betrayed. She saw the name in the letter. I showed it to her, damn it. Why didn't she say something then?"

Lara shook her head slowly, her expression bleak. "I'll tell you why, Duncan Stewart. Because I think my sweet friend was falling in love with you, and she couldn't believe that yet again her son-of-a-bitch, worthless father was ruining her life."

"You seem to know a lot about him."

"I should. Abby and I have been friends since we were in first grade. When I met her, she had already been without her mother for three years. A kid needs her mom, Duncan."

"Aye."

"I've watched that woman work twice as hard as everyone else for years. She always has to be the best. The smartest. The most prepared. She's loyal to a fault, and she would do anything for the people she cares about. For some reason, Duncan Stewart, that list most recently included you."

Duncan tasted shame, and his spirits sank lower. They had been driving for an hour already and had nothing to show for it. "Tell me about Howard Lander," he said. "We were at Abby's house one day, and she hid in the kitchen so she wouldn't have to answer the door."

Lara winced. "I tried to convince her to get a restraining order against him. She changed her name, but the legal action was a step too far."

"Maybe not now."

"True."

"What's wrong with the man?"

"Honestly, I don't know. He's too smart for his own good, for one thing. Abby has always tried to give him the benefit of the doubt. She thinks that losing her mother broke him."

"Or maybe he was always a jerk."

"Possibly. For years, he's been a functioning alcoholic. But lately, the act has worn thin. Did she ever tell you about last Christmas?"

"No. I've asked about her parents, but she didn't have much to say."

"It's no wonder. And for the record, my family has adopted her. We all love Abby, and if you mess with her again, we'll hurt you."

Duncan hid a faint smile. "Last Christmas? You were saying?"

Lara took a corner on two wheels. "Christmas Eve. Abby and I had been out to dinner with friends. We were on our way home when we cut through the town square in front of the courthouse. Howard was standing in the middle of the road wearing nothing but boxers, drunk out of his skull, singing Christmas carols."

"Hell."

"Yeah. It was pretty awful. The police carted him away, but the damage was done. Abby was humiliated. It was a human interest story, so one of the stations in Raleigh picked up the video footage and ran it on the evening news."

Duncan cursed. "I should press charges…send the bastard to jail. Would that make things better or worse?"

"I can't speak for Abby. Maybe that's something the two of you need to talk about."

Abby rotated her straightened-out coat hanger ninety degrees. Years ago, she had learned how to make the perfect s'more. The key was in a perfectly browned marshmallow. Her campfire was just right. Big enough to keep her warm. Not so big that she was risking a conflagration.

She knew Lara was worried about her. The texts had come fast and furious until Abby had been forced to turn off her phone. For the last twenty-plus hours, she'd been here at this campsite, hiding out. It was cowardly. She'd be the first to admit that. Even so, she needed time to recover.

Remembering the look on Duncan's face when he accused her of fraud still made her want to dive into a deep, dark hole. Forget having her heart broken. This was several levels worse.

She had the campsite mostly to herself. It was mid-week. The weather was nasty. Most of the tourists had moved on to other pursuits. Other than the fire, her only accoutrement was the portable awning that gave her a modicum of shelter from the elements. Fortunately, she had been able to snag the closest site to the bathhouse and the facilities.

Abby was car camping. It was something she and her dad used to do a lot when she was a kid. The childhood memories were happy ones. It was only much, much later that she realized they had been homeless for a time.

A gust of wind blew sideways, bringing a raw sluice of rain. She pulled her coat more tightly around her neck and stared into the flames. Her brain was blank. For the first time in many years, she had no clue how to move forward. Should she turn her father in to the authorities? Would that mean anything to Duncan?

The money was gone. No matter how many ways she tried to find a feasible solution, she hit a wall. She could work for the rest of her life and never be able to repay the Stewart family.

A sudden rustle of footsteps in the gravel brought her head up. Lara stood there, hands in the pockets of her raincoat. "You scared me, kid."

Abby grimaced. "Sorry."

She couldn't bring herself to look at the man beside Lara. But she glared at her friend. "Traitor."

Lara shrugged with an unrepentant smile. "I needed backup. He was available."

Duncan squatted and peered at Abby's dessert. "I'm no' an expert, but that looks revolting."

Lara thumped him on the shoulder. "When in Rome…" She leaned down and ruffled Abby's hair. "You want me to sit in the car? In case you need a referee?"

Abby grimaced and handed the coat hanger to Duncan. "No. You can go home." She stood and hugged her friend. "I don't know what to do," she whispered in Lara's ear, already close to tears again. And she *hated* that.

"*You* don't have to do anything, honey." Lara spoke softly so the words wouldn't travel to Duncan, especially with the rain pelting down. "The ball's in his court. If things get bad, call me and I'll be back in a flash."

Abby nodded, feeling nothing but a dull sense of dread. "Okay."

With nowhere else to go, she sat back down on the tarp.

Duncan shot her a sideways glance. "What am I holding?" he asked, staring at the sugary blob.

"Don't they have marshmallows in Scotland?"

"Aye. But we put them in cocoa. We don't incinerate them."

Abby reached in her waterproof tote and pulled out the graham crackers and Hershey's bars. "Give me a sec." She took the makeshift cooking utensil from him and held it over the fire again…only long enough to bring the marshmallow back to full heat. "Now, watch. Graham cracker. Chocolate. Hot marshmallow. And one more graham cracker. Voilà. A s'more."

"I'm missing something."

"It's a fun, gooey treat. And everyone always wants *some more*. Here. Try it."

Duncan's fingers brushed hers as she handed over the messy concoction. With a dubious expression, he opened his mouth and took a big bite. His eyes closed. She saw the moment the mélange of flavors hit his taste buds.

"Well?" she said. "What do you think?"

He wiped his mouth with the back of his hand. "You Americans have the weirdest and best ideas."

"So you like it?"

He nodded solemnly. "I do. But what about you? Shall I share this one?"

"I'll make another." She wanted something to occupy her hands and give her an excuse not to look at him. After threading a second fat marshmallow onto the coat hanger, she concentrated on her cooking.

Duncan finished his s'more and sat down cross-legged beside her on the tarp. He'd been squatting the entire time up until now. The man must have incredible thigh muscles.

Thinking about Duncan's thighs was not a good idea.

With her marshmallow nicely browned, she assembled her own dessert and took a bite. The knot in her chest relaxed as she stared into the flames. The scents and sounds of the fire made up for the fact that she couldn't feel her frozen feet. She'd been too upset to eat anything yesterday. Now she was starving.

Having Duncan with her here in the forest was both comforting and unsettling. Because she didn't know what to say, she kept quiet. He was quiet, as well.

The rain drummed on the tarp, providing an intimate, if somewhat damp, bubble of privacy.

Finally, Duncan sighed. He poked at the fire with a small stick, rearranging the coals and sending a geyser of sparks into the air. "I owe you an apology, Abby. I said things yesterday that I deeply regret."

She licked her fingers. "It's understandable. You were shocked and upset. And still grieving your grandmother."

He cursed beneath his breath. At least she thought it was a curse. The Gaelic word was unfamiliar.

He turned sideways and stared at her. "Are you always so quick to give people the benefit of the doubt? I'm sorry, Abby," he said. "Deeply sorry. I was angry with you for not telling me the truth, but it was more than that. From the beginning, I was conflicted about the fact that your firm had a client who wanted to buy the business. On the one hand, it seemed like my way out. But that felt disloyal to Granny. And then when I found out you had lied by omission, the whole thing seemed sinister."

"I'm sorry, too," she muttered. "My father—"

Duncan put a hand over her mouth. "We're not going to talk about him, Abby. He has nothing to do with you and me. His sins are his own. You have nothing to be ashamed of, nothing at all. It's not your fault."

"Then why do I feel so terrible?" she croaked. There was nothing she could do about the tear that rolled down her cheek.

Duncan scooted closer and put his arm around her. The heat from his big body was more comforting than the fire. "It's time for me to talk and you to listen, lass. Can you do that?"

She nodded. Whatever he was going to tell her was bound to be painful, but she was a big girl. Closure was good.

Duncan took her chin without warning. "Ye've got marshmallow on your cheek. Hold still."

She held her breath as he bent and kissed away the sticky, sweet residue. His lips never touched hers. But he was so close she could feel the stubble on his face. The man hadn't shaved. And now that she thought about it, he looked like someone who hadn't slept in days.

Her heart raced. Her blood pumped.

Maybe she was experiencing a sugar high. That's all.

Duncan retreated and tucked her more firmly against his side. "I've not been entirely honest with you, Abby."

Alarm skittered through her veins. Was there a woman in his life after all? "Oh?" she said, trying not to sound as freaked out as she felt.

"I resented the hell out of the fact that I had to be the one to come here to the States and help Granny run Stewart Properties. I felt backed into a corner by circumstances beyond my control."

"I see."

"My life in Skye was good. *Is* good," he said firmly. "I like my job and my friends and the vast, wild beauty of the land where I grew up."

Her heart sank. "I see." It was the only response she could come up with, at least the only one that didn't reveal too much of her own distress.

"I don't think you do," he said slowly. "My life in Skye is great. It's *comfortable*. But here's the thing, Abby. I'm thirty-two years old. I don't think *comfortable* is the endgame for a man my age. That's for people who are fifty or sixty or, hell, I don't know. Maybe even eighty."

"What are you trying to say, Duncan?"

He ran a hand through his hair. "The TV shrinks tell us that personal growth only happens when we're pushed outside our comfort zones. Well, I'm here to tell you that these last couple of months have been *way* the hell out of my comfort zone. And what's worse, even after I made the decision to move to Candlewick and help, suddenly Granny was dead. And the business had lost five million dollars…and—"

When he ground to a halt, she saw the muscles in his throat work. Against hers, his body was rigid.

"What, Duncan? And what?"

He turned and pressed a kiss to her temple. "And then there was you."

To be included in his list of tragedies stung. "I'm sorry I made your life difficult," she said.

His rough laugh held little real humor. "You were the only bright spot in a very traumatic season for me. You were charming and funny, and then later… Well, you were my friend, Abby. And finally, my lover. My feelings for you have been all wrapped up in the upheaval of my comfortable life, and I haven't had a clue what to do about you."

Her heart sank. Duncan's honesty was hard to bear. She was glad he didn't blame her for the missing money, but the man was not exactly pledging his undying love. How could he? They'd known each other less than a month.

Suddenly, the rain went from gentle showers to a deluge. Huge, fat droplets pummeled the fire, making it sizzle and pop.

Even the overhead canopy wasn't sufficient to keep them dry.

Abby took his hand. "We need to get in the car," she said. She made a dash for the vehicle, opened it and scrambled into the back, waiting for him to follow. Duncan was right on her heels. He slammed the door and sprawled in the seat with a sigh. "Where's your tent, lass?"

"Don't have one. I slept right here last night." She pulled a tissue from her pocket and dried her face. There was nothing she could do about her hair. From past experience, she knew her curls were running wild. She didn't have on a lick of makeup, and her T-shirt and jeans were ancient. This might be the last time she ever saw Duncan Stewart, and she looked like hell.

With all the car doors shut, the windows soon steamed up from their breathing. A big man like Duncan Stewart put off a lot of body heat.

Despite being wet and exhausted, he looked ruggedly handsome. It really wasn't fair.

She summoned her courage. "There's no need to

worry about me, Duncan. I knew when I first kissed you that we were having a fling. I guess since it's you, that makes it a Highland fling?" She was getting punchy from lack of sleep and grief and the strain of not begging him to stay.

He frowned. "Listen. Don't talk. Remember?"

She mimed zipping her lips.

Duncan's lips quirked in a half smile. "So to sum up, these last few weeks have set me on my heels. Every time I thought I had found solid ground, something else happened to shove me on my ass. When I thought Granny was leaving the company to Brody and me fifty-fifty, it was bad enough. But then you told me about the damned will and all the changes, and suddenly all of this was *my* responsibility. The business. The house. The family heritage."

"Well, not to beat a dead horse, but with a few strokes of a pen, you can be done with it all. You can be home in Scotland before you know it. No more responsibility. No more ties."

"And no more you." He said it soberly.

Her eyes stung. "This is a really long speech. And my clothes are wet. Could we speed this up, please?"

Duncan laughed out loud. "God, I adore you."

"You do?" She blinked at him, wondering if the water in her ears had affected her hearing.

"Come here, my sweet, wet Abby." He pulled her into his embrace and stretched out as much as he could with her on top of him in a very compromising fashion. "Kiss me, love."

Then his hand was on the back of her neck and their lips met and every inch of her body that had been cold and shivering moments before was now on fire.

Duncan tasted like chocolate and marshmallows and everything she had ever wanted in her life. His tongue teased her lips, stroking and thrusting and taking her breath.

"I don't know why we're doing this," she said, half-panicked.

"I do," he groaned. He slid a hand under her shirt and unfastened her bra. His fingers teased her taut nipples. "You gave yourself to me, lass. Body and soul. I took the gift, and I didn't treasure it, but I won't make that mistake again." He cupped one of her breasts and squeezed gently.

"Finish your speech," she said, breathless with hope.

He smiled and kissed her nose. A giant sigh lifted his chest and let it fall again. He tucked her head against his shoulder. "I'm not leaving Candlewick, Abby. I'm not leaving you. It finally dawned on me that what I really want is to carry on my grandparents' legacy. I think it's my purpose. The missing money may be more of a blow than I realize, but I'm not afraid of hard work. And there's one more thing..."

She held her breath, playing with his collarbone where she had unbuttoned his shirt. "Yes?"

"I want you to do it with me," he said firmly. "Either formally or informally. If you want to continue your job at the law firm, I certainly understand. But I would think a company like ours could use professional legal counsel in-house. Under the circumstances, I'm not sure what kind of salary I can offer you, but the benefits package would be significant."

She stroked him through the heavy, damp denim that was not thick enough to disguise the eagerness of his erection. "I'm impressed by your package already," she teased. The reality of what he was saying overrode the humor in the situation. Her chin wobbled. "You're serious about this?"

He held her chin with two fingers, tilting her head so he could see her face. His gentle gaze held so much pure emotion, her heart contracted. "I've never been more sure of anything, Abby. I want you to be my wife. I love you body and soul. And before you even have to ask, that means children, too."

Suddenly, everything she had ever wanted was a breath away. It seemed too good to be true. Her entire body trembled with a mixture of fear and delight. "You love me? Truly?"

Seventeen

Duncan stroked her hair, feeling the silky, bouncy waves. "To my very bones. We're going to call this a practice proposal. It's too soon, and I want you to know you can trust me for the long haul." He paused and winced. "Not to mention the fact that I'd prefer a more romantic setting."

"Ah, a Scotsman with a heart for romance. If we ever get married, will you promise to wear your kilt?"

He pinched her butt. "No *ifs* about it, lass. You're mine now. No going back. And yes. I'll be delighted to wear my kilt if it will make you happy."

She lifted up, bracing her hand on his chest. "*You* make me happy, Duncan. I love you."

"Even though I was a damned fool yesterday? I let my pride and my prejudices get in the way, and I nearly lost you. I'll no' ever get over that. I was arrogant, Abby. I thought I knew how to handle Granny, how to handle the business, hell, even how to handle you. I thought all I wanted was a temporary affair. But I was wrong on so many levels."

"That's in the past. We're looking toward the future."

He raked a hand through her curls, toying with them as they wrapped around his fingers. "Our vehicles are smaller in Scotland. But I've heard 'tis a rite of passage for an American lass to give herself to the man she loves in the back seat of a car."

"Not at our age. We have two perfectly good houses at our disposal."

His breathing came faster. He unbuttoned her jeans and slid his hands inside. "Can't wait."

Duncan recognized the complicated logistics. But he had Abby in his arms again, and it felt as if it had been weeks since he last made love to her. He nuzzled her neck. "What if I sit up and you straddle my lap?" The rain was a torrent now, ensuring that no prying eyes would spot them, not to mention the fact that Abby's car was the only one anywhere around.

Her eyes widened. A pink flush suffused her throat and cheeks. "I don't know…"

"Don't be bashful, sweet girl. I won't let anything happen to you."

His proposition meant that Abby had to shed her clothing completely, at least from the waist down. He helped her undress with barely controlled impatience, pausing to kiss and stroke and fondle until they were both shaking and clumsy with hunger.

When everything was right, Duncan found the single condom he'd had the foresight to bring along and rolled it on. Steadying Abby with his hands at her waist, he eased her down on top of him. Her body accepted his urgent possession. He filled her with a ragged thrust and a groan.

She rested her forehead against his. "I would go to Scotland if you asked me, Duncan. I don't want you to have regrets."

He wheezed out a laugh, barely able to breathe. "Don't be daft. *This* is what I want. As long as I have you, I have everything."

That she could forgive him so easily for his cruel accusations the day before made him want to be a better man. God willing, he had years ahead to prove to her that her trust in him was not misplaced. With everything he had, he would honor and protect her.

A family would be nice. A boy. And then a girl.

His orgasm bore down on him, demanding, importunate.

Duncan gritted his teeth and concentrated on Abby. He reached between them and touched her intimately. The sight of their joined bodies affected him profoundly. Whatever his sins in the past, he must have done something right to deserve this woman.

Abby clung to his neck. Her breasts mashed up against his chest, making him dizzy. She bit his earlobe, her breath tickling his ear. "I'm close," she whispered. "Give me everything. Send me over."

She didn't have to ask twice. With a roar of exultation, he braced his feet against the floor of the car, gripped her hips and thrust again and again until his vision went black and Abby cried out his name.

Eons later, he realized that his lover's cute bottom was cold. He didn't want to move. His body was lax with pleasure, his brain clearer and more calm than it had been in months.

He blew a curl out of his face. "Anybody awake in there?"

Abby pulled back, sending delightful aftershocks through his sex. Her smile was tremulous. "You do that really well."

"I don't know what you mean," he said, straight-faced. "This is my first time to shag in a car."

"Very funny."

"I try," he said modestly. He sensed the moment when her mood changed.

She sobered, her hands braced on his shoulders. "Things always seem perfect when we're having sex, but our world is complicated, Duncan. My father will always be my father. I can't make him go away. If you're living in Candlewick, you'll be bound to run into him sooner than later."

Instead of answering, Duncan eased Abby off of him and helped her deal with her clothes. When they were both decent again, he caught her close for a hard kiss. "It doesn't matter," he said. "And for the record, I won't be pressing any charges. For one thing, it would be difficult to prove anything in court. My grandfather withdrew the money of his own free will. But more than that, legal action would be pointless because there is no money to recoup. And it would hurt you. We can see him or not see him. He helped give birth to you, so I'm feeling remarkably mellow about all that right now. But it's your call."

Abby leaned her head against his shoulder and reached up to kiss him. "Thank you."

Her gratitude bothered him. "Don't thank me." His

throat tightened. "I don't know if I can forgive myself for attacking you yesterday. I knew in my gut what kind of woman you are. You never lied to me about anything that truly mattered. I was hung up on my pride and my fear of betrayal. I let myself be blinded by evidence that didn't add up. I won't ever do that to you again, I swear."

"Stop it, Duncan," she said firmly. "It was a crisis, and we all make mistakes under pressure. I should have told you immediately that he was my father. So I screwed up, too. No more sadness. Not today."

He held her close, marveling at what life had given him. "I wish Granny had lived to see you and me together."

"I like to believe she *does* know. She and your grandfather both." She smiled against his chest, her cheek resting right over his heart. "I think I'm going to like being a Stewart."

"Well, lass, the Stewarts are the lucky ones. Because they have you." He tilted her chin up and found her lips with a kiss that threatened to start round two. "And so do I..."

Epilogue

Duncan ran both hands through his hair and tried to swallow the knot in his throat. "Well, how do I look?"

Brody snickered. "I've never seen you like this, little brother. It's pretty damned funny."

"Shut up and help me. We have to walk out there in about a minute and a half. Is my jacket collar straight?"

Both men were wearing full dress kilts at Abby's request. In the same church where the Stewart funerals had been conducted, Duncan would now pledge eternal devotion to his bride.

In the distance, the plaintive sounds of a bagpipe echoed.

Brody, taking Duncan by surprise, hugged his brother tightly. "I'm going to miss you, damn it. But

I know you're doing the right thing. Granny and Grandda would be delighted and proud."

Duncan nodded, his throat tight. "Ye know I'm not staying here in Candlewick out of obligation... right? I want this. For me. For Abby. For future generations of Stewarts."

"I can't think of a better way to start your life together."

The door adjacent to the altar opened, and the minister gave them a nod. The men strode into the sanctuary, barely registering the rustle of response at their appearance.

The church was decked out for Christmas with poinsettias in the windows and swags of fragrant balsam everywhere.

Down the center aisle, a local piper strolled, playing a traditional tune. Behind him, clad in dark green velvet, Abby's friend Lara walked slowly. At the back of the church, framed in the doorway, stood the only person Duncan wanted to see.

Abby was wearing a traditional wedding gown. Knowing how much she had missed in her young life, Duncan had insisted she have all the bells and whistles for this wedding. She carried a bouquet of crimson roses and eucalyptus.

Her dress was strapless and cut low over her beautiful breasts. An antique lace veil flowed from a diamond tiara that had been part of Duncan's wedding gift to her, along with a simple teardrop necklace that matched the headpiece.

As she walked down the aisle toward him, everything in the room faded away until all he could see was his Abby. Beautiful gray eyes met his. Everything she was—her spirit, her integrity, her huge caring heart—shone in that gaze.

Lara took her place opposite Brody.

Then it was time for Abby to ascend the shallow steps. Duncan gripped her hand to help her, kissed her cheek and wrapped her arm through his as they took their assigned places. "I love you," he said, going off script.

The chuckle that ran through the crowd barely registered.

Abby looked up at him, her eyes bright with tears. "And I love you, stubborn Scotsman. Now hush and let the minister do his job. We have a lifetime ahead of us for kissing."

Duncan glanced at Brody and grinned. Then he took a deep breath and squeezed his bride-to-be's arm, focusing obediently on the officiant. "Aye, love, that we do."

* * * * *

From New York Times *bestselling author Maisey Yates comes the sizzling second book in her new* GOLD VALLEY *Western romance series. Shy tomboy Kaylee Capshaw never thought she'd have a chance of winning the heart of her longtime friend Bennett Dodge, even if he is the cowboy of her dreams.*

But when she learns he's suddenly single, can she finally prove to him that the woman he's been waiting for has been right here all along?

Read on for a sneak peek at UNTAMED COWBOY, *the latest in* New York Times *bestselling author Maisey Yates's* GOLD VALLEY *series!*

CHAPTER ONE

KAYLEE CAPSHAW NEEDED a new life. Which was why she was steadfastly avoiding the sound of her phone vibrating in her purse while the man across from her at the beautifully appointed dinner table continued to talk, oblivious to the internal war raging inside of her.

Do not look at your phone.

The stern internal admonishment didn't help. Everything in her was still seized up with adrenaline and anxiety over the fact that she had texts she wasn't looking at.

Not because of her job. Any and all veterinary emergencies were being covered by her new assistant at the clinic, Laura, so that she could have this date with Michael, the perfectly nice man she was now ignoring while she warred within herself to *not look down at her phone.*

No. It wasn't work texts she was itching to look at.

But what if it was Bennett?

Laura knew that she wasn't supposed to interrupt Kaylee tonight, because Kaylee was on a date, but she had conveniently not told Bennett. Because she didn't want to talk to Bennett about her dating anyone.

Mostly because she didn't want to hear if Bennett was dating anyone. If the woman lasted, Kaylee would inevitably know all about her. So there was no reason—in her mind—to rush into all of that.

She wasn't going to look at her phone.

"Going over the statistical data for the last quarter was really very interesting. It's fascinating how the holidays inform consumers."

Kaylee blinked. "What?"

"Sorry. I'm probably boring you. The corporate side of retail at Christmas is probably only interesting to people who work in the industry."

"Not at all," she said. Except, she wasn't interested. But she was trying to be. "How exactly did you get involved in this job living here?"

"Well, I can do most of it online. Sometimes I travel to Portland, which is where the corporate office is." Michael worked for a world-famous brand of sports gear, and he did something with the sales. Or data.

Her immediate attraction to him had been his dachshund, Clarence, whom she had seen for a tooth abscess a couple of weeks earlier. Then on a follow-up visit, he had asked if Kaylee would like to go out, and she had honestly not been able to think of one good reason she shouldn't. Except for Bennett Dodge. Her best friend since junior high and the obsessive focus of her hormones since she'd discovered what men and women did together in the dark.

Which meant she absolutely needed to go out with Michael.

Bennett couldn't be the excuse. Not anymore.

She had fallen into a terrible rut over the last couple of years while she and Bennett had gotten their clinic up and running. Work and her social life revolved around him. Social gatherings were all linked to him and to his family.

She'd lived in Gold Valley since junior high, and the friendships she'd made here had mostly faded since then. She'd made friends when she'd gone to school for veterinary medicine, but she and Bennett had gone together, and those friends were mostly mutual friends.

If they ever came to town for a visit, it included Bennett. If she took a trip to visit them, it often included Bennett.

The man was up in absolutely everything, and the effects of it had been magnified recently as her world had narrowed thanks to their mutually demanding work schedule.

That amount of intense, focused time with him never failed to put her in a somewhat pathetic emotional space.

Hence the very necessary date.

Then her phone started vibrating because it was ringing, and she couldn't ignore that. "I'm sorry," she said. "Excuse me."

It was Bennett. Her heart slammed into her throat. She should not answer it. She really shouldn't. She thought that even while she was pressing the green accept button.

"What's up?" she asked.

"Calving drama. I have a breech one. I need some help."

Bennett sounded clipped and stressed. And he didn't stress easily. He delivered countless calves over the course of the season, but a breech birth was never good. If the rancher didn't call him in time, there was rarely anything that could be done.

And if Bennett needed some assistance, then the situation was probably pretty extreme.

"Where are you?" she asked, darting a quick look over to Michael and feeling like a terrible human for being marginally relieved by this interruption.

"Out of town at Dave Miller's place. Follow the driveway out back behind the house."

"See you soon." She hung up the phone and looked down at her half-finished dinner. "I am so sorry," she said, forcing herself to look at Michael's face. "There's a veterinary emergency. I have to go."

She stood up, collecting her purse and her jacket. "I really am sorry. I tried to cover everything. But my partner... It's a barnyard thing. He needs help."

Michael looked... Well, he looked understanding. And Kaylee almost wished that he wouldn't. That he would be mad so that she would have an excuse to storm off and never have dinner with him again. That he would be unreasonable in some fashion so that she could call the date experiment a loss and go back to making no attempts at a romantic life whatsoever.

But he didn't. "Of course," he said. "You can't let something happen to an animal just because you're on a dinner date."

"I really can't," she said. "I'm sorry."

She reached into her purse and pulled out a twenty-dollar bill. She put it on the table and offered an apologetic smile before turning and leaving. Before he didn't accept her contribution to the dinner.

She was not going to make him pay for the entire meal on top of everything.

"Have a good evening," the hostess said as Kaylee walked toward the front door of the restaurant. "Please dine with us again soon."

Kaylee muttered something and headed outside, stumbling a little bit when her kitten heel caught in a crack in the sidewalk. That was the highest heel she ever wore, since she was nearly six feet tall in flats, and towering over one's date was not the best first impression.

But she was used to cowgirl boots and not these spindly, fiddly things that hung up on every imperfection. They were impractical. How any woman walked around in stilettos was beyond her.

The breeze kicked up, reminding her that March could not be counted on for warm spring weather as the wind stung her bare legs. The cost of wearing a dress. Which also had her feeling pretty stupid right about now.

She always felt weird in dresses, owing that to her stick figure and excessive height. She'd had to be tough from an early age. With parents who ultimately ended up ignoring her existence, she'd had to be self-sufficient.

It had suited her to be a tomboy because spending time outdoors, running around barefoot and climbing trees, far away from the fight scenes her parents continually staged in their house, was better than sitting at home.

Better to pretend she didn't like lace and frills,

since her bedroom consisted of a twin mattress on the floor and a threadbare afghan.

She'd had a friend when she was little, way before they'd moved to Gold Valley, who'd had the prettiest princess room on earth. Lace bedding, a canopy. Pink walls with flower stencils. She'd been so envious of it. She'd felt nearly sick with it.

But she'd just said she hated girlie things. And never invited that friend over ever.

And hey, she'd been built for it. Broad shoulders and stuff.

Sadly, she *wasn't* built for pretty dresses.

But she needed strength more, anyway.

She was thankful she had driven her own truck, which was parked not far down the street against the curb. First-date rule for her. Drive your own vehicle. In case you had to make a hasty getaway.

And apparently she had needed to make a hasty getaway, just not because Michael was a weirdo or anything.

No, he had been distressingly nice.

She mused on that as she got into the driver's seat and started the engine. She pulled away from the curb and headed out of town. Yes, he had been perfectly nice. Really, there had been nothing wrong with him. And she was a professional at finding things wrong with the men she went on dates with. A professional at finding excuses for why a second date couldn't possibly happen.

She was ashamed to realize now that she was hoping he would consider this an excuse not to make a second date with her.

That she had taken a phone call in the middle of dinner and then had run off.

A lot of people had trouble dating. But often it was for deep reasons they had trouble identifying.

Kaylee knew exactly why she had trouble dating.

It was because she was in love with her best friend, Bennett Dodge. And he was *not* in love with her.

She gritted her teeth.

She wasn't in love with Bennett. No. She wouldn't allow that. She had lustful feelings for Bennett, and she cared deeply about him. But she wasn't in love with him. She refused to let it be that. Not anymore.

That thought carried her over the gravel drive that led to the ranch, back behind the house, just as Bennett had instructed. The doors to the barn were flung open, the lights on inside, and she recognized Bennett's truck parked right outside.

She killed the engine and got out, then moved into the barn as quickly as possible.

"What's going on?" she asked.

Dave Miller was there, his arms crossed over his chest, standing back against the wall. Bennett had his hand on the cow's back. He turned to look at her, the overhead light in the barn seeming to shine a halo around his cowboy hat. That chiseled face that she knew so well but never failed to make her stomach go tight. He stroked the cow, his large, capable hands drawing her attention, as well as the muscles in his forearm. He was wearing a tight T-shirt that showed off the play of those muscles to perfection. His large biceps and the scars on his skin from various on-the-job injuries. He had a stethoscope draped over his shoulders, and something about that combination—rough-and-

ready cowboy meshed with concerned veterinarian—
was her very particular catnip.

"I need to get the calf out as quickly as possible,
and I need to do it at the right moment. Too quickly
and we're likely to crush the baby's ribs." She had a
feeling he said that part for the benefit of the nervous-
looking rancher standing off to the side.

Dave Miller was relatively new to town, having
moved up from California a couple of years ago with
fantasies of rural living. A small ranch for him and
his wife's retirement had grown to a medium-sized
one over the past year or so. And while the older man
had a reputation for taking great care of his animals,
he wasn't experienced at this.

"Where do you want me?" she asked, moving over
to where Bennett was standing.

"I'm going to need you to suction the hell out of
this thing as soon as I get her out." He appraised her.
"Where were you?"

"It doesn't matter."

"You're wearing a dress."

She shrugged. "I wasn't at home."

He frowned. "Were you out?"

This was not the time for Bennett to go overly
concerned big brother on her. It wasn't charming on
a normal day, but it was even less charming when
she'd just abandoned her date to help deliver a calf.
"If I wasn't at home, I was out. Better put your hand
up the cow, Bennett," she said, feeling testy.

Bennett did just that, checking to see that the cow
was dilated enough for him to extract the calf. Deliv-
ering a breech animal like this was tricky business.
They were going to have to pull the baby out, likely

with the aid of a chain or a winch, but not *too* soon, which would injure the mother. And not too quickly, which would injure them both.

But if they went too slow, the baby cow would end up completely cut off from its oxygen supply. If that happened, it was likely to never recover.

"Ready," he said. "I need chains."

She looked around and saw the chains lying on the ground, then she picked them up and handed them over. He grunted and pulled, producing the first hint of the calf's hooves. Then he lashed the chain around them. He began to pull again, his muscles straining against the fabric of his black T-shirt, flexing as he tugged hard.

She had been a vet long enough that she was inured to things like this, from a gross-out-factor perspective. But still, checking out a guy in the midst of all of this was probably a little imbalanced. Of course, that was the nature of how things were with her and Bennett.

They'd met when she'd moved to Gold Valley at thirteen—all long limbs, anger and adolescent awkwardness. And somehow, they'd fit. He'd lost his mother when he was young, and his family was limping along. Her own home life was hard, and she'd been desperate for escape from her parents' neglect and drunken rages at each other.

She never had him over. She didn't want to be at her house. She never wanted him, or any other friend, to see the way her family lived.

To see her sad mattress on the floor and her peeling nightstand.

Instead, they'd spent time at the Dodge ranch. His

family had become hers, in many ways. They weren't perfect, but there was more love in their broken pieces than Kaylee's home had ever had.

He'd taught her to ride horses, let her play with the barn cats and the dogs that lived on the ranch. Together, the two of them had saved a baby squirrel that had been thrown out of his nest, nursing him back to health slowly in a little shoebox.

She'd blossomed because of him. Had discovered her love of animals. And had discovered she had the power to fix some of the broken things in the world.

The two of them had decided to become veterinarians together after they'd successfully saved the squirrel. And Bennett had never wavered.

He was a constant. A sure and steady port in the storm of life.

And when her feelings for him had started to shift and turn into more, she'd done her best to push them down because he was her whole world, and she didn't want to risk that by introducing anything as volatile as romance.

She'd seen how that went. Her parents' marriage was a reminder of just how badly all that could sour. It wasn't enough to make her swear off men, but it was enough to make her want to keep her relationship with Bennett as it was.

But that didn't stop the attraction.

If it were as simple as deciding not to want him, she would have done it a long time ago. And if it were as simple as being with another man, that would have worked back in high school when she had committed to finding herself a prom date and losing her virginity so she could get over Bennett Dodge already.

It had not worked. And the sex had been disappointing.

So here she was, fixating on his muscles while he helped an animal give birth.

Maybe there wasn't a direct line between those two things, but sometimes it felt like it. If all other men could just…not be so disappointing in comparison to Bennett Dodge, things would be much easier.

She looked away from him, making herself useful, gathering syringes and anything she would need to clear the calf of mucus that might be blocking its airway. Bennett hadn't said anything, likely for Dave's benefit, but she had a feeling he was worried about the health of the heifer. That was why he needed her to see to the calf as quickly as possible, because he was afraid he would be giving treatment to its mother.

She spread a blanket out that was balled up and stuffed in the corner—unnecessary, but it was something to do. Bennett strained and gave one final pull and brought the calf down as gently as possible onto the barn floor.

"There he is," Bennett said, breathing heavily. "There he is."

His voice was filled with that rush of adrenaline that always came when they worked jobs like this.

She and Bennett ran the practice together, but she typically held down the fort at the clinic and treated smaller domestic animals like birds, dogs, cats and the occasional ferret.

Bennett worked with large animals, cows, horses, goats and sometimes llamas. They had a mobile unit for things like this.

But when push came to shove, they helped each other out.

And when push came to pulling a calf out of its mother, they definitely helped each other.

Bennett took care of the cord and then turned his focus back to the mother.

Kaylee moved to the calf, who was glassy-eyed and not looking very good. But she knew from her limited experience with this kind of delivery that just because they came out like this didn't mean they wouldn't pull through.

She checked his airway, brushing away any remaining mucus that was in the way. She put her hand back over his midsection and tried to get a feel on his heartbeat. "Bennett," she said, "stethoscope?"

"Here," he said, taking it from around his neck and tossing it her direction. She caught it and slipped the ear tips in, then pressed the diaphragm against the calf, trying to get a sense of what was happening in there.

His heartbeat sounded strong, which gave her hope.

His breathing was still weak. She looked around at the various tools, trying to see something she might be able to use. "Dave," she said to the man standing back against the wall. "I need a straw."

"A straw?"

"Yes. I've never tried this before, but I hear it works."

She had read that sticking a straw up a calf's nose irritated the system enough that it jolted them into breathing. And she hoped that was the case.

Dave returned quickly with the item that she had

requested, and Kaylee moved the straw into position. Not gently, since that would defeat the purpose.

You had to love animals to be in her line of work. And unfortunately, loving them sometimes meant hurting them.

The calf startled, then heaved, his chest rising and falling deeply before he started to breathe quickly.

Kaylee pulled the straw out and lifted her hands. "Thank God."

Bennett turned around, shifting his focus to the calf and away from the mother. "Breathing?"

"Breathing."

He nodded, wiping his forearm over his forehead. "Good." His chest pitched upward sharply. "I think Mom is going to be okay, too."

***

UNTAMED COWBOY
by New York Times *bestselling author*
Maisey Yates,
available July 2018 wherever
HQN Books and ebooks are sold.
www.Harlequin.com

Get 4 FREE REWARDS!

We'll send you 2 FREE Books <u>plus</u> 2 FREE Mystery Gifts.

Harlequin® Desire books feature heroes who have it all: wealth, status, incredible good looks... everything but the right woman.

FREE Value Over **$20**

SPECIAL EXCERPT FROM

(H)HARLEQUIN® *Desire*

*Wealthy Texas politician Chase Ferguson ended things with his
ex to protect her. Yet now she's crashed his isolated vacation
house in a snowstorm. And when a stormbound seduction has
real-world repercussions, he must make a stand for what—and
who—he truly believes in.*

*Read on for a sneak peek at
A Snowbound Scandal by Jessica Lemmon,
part of her **Dallas Billionaires Club** series!*

Her mouth watered, not for the food, but for him.

Not why you came here, Miriam reminded herself sternly.

Yet here she stood. Chase had figured out—before she'd
admitted it to herself—that she'd come here not only to give
him a piece of her mind but also to give herself the comfort of
knowing he'd had a home-cooked meal on Thanksgiving.

She balled her fist as a flutter of desire took flight between her
thighs. She wanted to touch him. Maybe just once.

He pushed her wineglass closer to her. An offer.

An offer she wouldn't accept.

Couldn't accept.

She wasn't unlike Little Red Riding Hood, having run to the
wrong house for shelter. Only in this case, the Big Bad Wolf
wasn't dining on Red's beloved grandmother but Miriam's
family's home cooking.

An insistent niggling warned her that she could be next—and
hadn't this particular "wolf" already consumed her heart?

"So, I'm going to go."

When she grabbed her coat and stood, a warm hand grasped
her much cooler one. Chase's fingers stroked hers before lightly

squeezing, his eyes studying her for a long moment, his fork hovering over his unfinished dinner.

Finally, he said, "I'll see you out."

"That's not necessary."

He did as he pleased and stood, his hand on her lower back as he walked with her. Outside, the wind pushed against the front door, causing the wood to creak. She and Chase exchanged glances. Had she waited too long?

"For the record, I don't want you to leave."

What she'd have given to hear those words on that airfield ten years ago.

"I'll be all right."

"You can't know that." He frowned out of either concern or anger, she couldn't tell which.

"Stay." Chase's gray-green eyes were warm and inviting, his voice a time capsule back to not-so-innocent days. The request was siren-call sweet, but she'd not risk herself for it.

"No." She yanked open the front door, shocked when the howling wind shoved her back a few inches. Snow billowed in, swirling around her feet, and her now wet, cold fingers slipped from the knob.

Chase caught her, an arm looped around her back, and shoved the door closed with the flat of one palm. She hung there, suspended by the corded forearm at her back, clutching his shirt in one fist, and nearly drowned in his lake-colored eyes.

"I can stay for a while longer," she squeaked, the decision having been made for her.

His handsome face split into a brilliant smile.

Don't miss A Snowbound Scandal *by Jessica Lemmon,*
part of her **Dallas Billionaires Club** *series!*

Available August 2018 wherever
Harlequin® Desire books and ebooks are sold.

www.Harlequin.com

Want to give in to temptation with
steamy tales of irresistible desire?

Check out **Harlequin® Presents®,
Harlequin® Desire** and
Harlequin® Kimani™ Romance books!

New books available every month!

LOVE
Harlequin
romance?

Join our Harlequin community to share your thoughts and connect with other romance readers!

Be the first to find out about promotions, news, and exclusive content!

Sign up for the Harlequin e-newsletter and download a free book from any series at

www.TryHarlequin.com

CONNECT WITH US AT:

Harlequin.com/Community

 Facebook.com/HarlequinBooks

 Twitter.com/HarlequinBooks

 Instagram.com/HarlequinBooks

 Pinterest.com/HarlequinBooks

ReaderService.com

**ROMANCE WHEN
YOU NEED IT**

THE WORLD IS WITH

Romance

Harlequin has everything from contemporary, passionate and heartwarming to suspenseful and inspirational stories.

Whatever your mood, we have a romance just for you!

Connect with us to find your next great read, special offers and more.

f /HarlequinBooks

🐦 @HarlequinBooks

www.HarlequinBlog.com

www.Harlequin.com/Newsletters

H HARLEQUIN®

A *Romance* FOR EVERY MOOD™

www.Harlequin.com

SERIESHALOAD2015